AFTER THE FALL

By

Ellis Grayson

After the Fall
Copyright © 2025 Ellis Grayson

All rights reserved.

Prologue

The world ended not with a bang, but a slow, relentless crawl.

Once, cities thrived with life and laughter now, only silence and shadows remain. The dead walk, minds lost to a merciless hunger, and the living fight not just for survival, but for hope.

In the ruins of humanity, two communities cling to fragile peace. But beneath the surface, old wounds and new dangers threaten to tear them apart. As the battle for the future looms, alliances will be tested, secrets will surface, and sacrifices will be made.

This is their story. This is what happens After the Fall.

Chapter 1: Echoes of the Old World

The sky over Blantyre was a dull grey blanket, thick with smoke and silence. Once a bustling town of life and laughter, now only wind and ash dared move freely through its broken streets. Six months had passed since the world ended, and the dead still walked.

Derek crouched behind a crumbled stone wall near the High Blantyre primary school, his knuckles white around the grip of a blood-smeared fire axe. Sweat dripped from his brow despite the chill in the air. Beside him, Jennifer silently loaded another magazine into her pistol, her eyes flicking between the street ahead and the alley behind them.

"Movement, two zombies, maybe three," whispered Callum, peeking over the top of the wall through a pair of cracked binoculars. His face was gaunt, beard overgrown, but the fire in his eyes burned hotter than ever.

Anne leaned against the wall, a makeshift spear in her hands. "We need that food drop. If we don't get it today, we're not seeing tomorrow."

Jennifer nodded. "Then we do it quietly. In and out. No heroics."

A low groan echoed down the street the unmistakable moan of the dead. One of them had caught their scent.

Derek stood. "No time for quiet anymore." He stepped over the wall and charged. Derek's boots hit the cracked pavement hard. The fire axe felt heavy, but familiar. He gritted his teeth as the first zombie came into view, a gaunt man in a shredded Tesco uniform, its head lolling unnaturally to one side. It let out a low groan and reached for him with filthy, bloodstained hands.

He swung.

The axe buried deep into the skull with a sickening crunch. Derek yanked it free, barely missing the second zombie as it lurched toward him, arms wide like a twisted embrace. Behind him, Callum vaulted the wall and tackled the creature, driving his hunting knife up through its jaw. The body collapsed in a heap.

Jennifer followed a split second later, already scanning for threats. "Two more, ten o'clock!" she called, raising her pistol. Two quick pops one missed, the other took out the lead zombie's knee. It crumpled, still crawling, snarling.

Anne circled wide, jabbing her spear into the throat of another. She grimaced as blood sprayed across her coat, but she held firm. The creature gurgled, then stilled.

"Clear!" Callum shouted.

They stood in the silence that followed, chests heaving, surrounded by the twitching corpses of what used to be neighbors. The wind whistled through broken windows and the smell of rot clung to everything.

Derek wiped his axe on a tattered bit of clothing. "That was too close. They're getting thicker."

Jennifer pointed to the old community centre a few blocks down. "Food crate's inside. That flare last night came from the roof."

"Or it's a trap," Anne muttered.

Callum gave a grim smile. "Only one way to find out."

Derek nodded. "Let's move. Fast and tight. If we're lucky, we'll be back at the school before dark."

They took off down the street, weapons ready, eyes scanning every shadow. In this new world, hope was just another word for bait and the dead never stopped hunting. The community centre loomed ahead, its faded sign hanging askew above the double doors. A burnt-out police van sat in the car park, half-eaten corpses still slumped inside. Windows were shattered. Blood smears decorated the walls like grotesque murals. Whatever had happened here, it hadn't been quiet. Derek crouched by the entrance and motioned for the others to stack up behind him. "Anne cover the left. Callum, check our six. Jen, on me."

Jennifer gave a tight nod, eyes hard. She holstered her pistol and unslung a small crowbar from her pack.

Quiet was the goal if the building was full of zombies, they didn't need to wake them all.

The door creaked as it opened, revealing a dim hallway lined with broken chairs and smeared handprints. A child's toy, a plastic dump truck lay on its side, wheels still spinning slightly in the breeze.

The silence was wrong.

Derek stepped inside first, moving low and slow. The group followed, weapons raised. Their boots barely made a sound on the bloodstained linoleum.

They passed a smashed vending machine, shattered glass crunching underfoot. Then a noise. A distant, dragging shuffle. Somewhere deeper inside.

Jennifer whispered, "South wing. Gymnasium maybe."

"That's where the flare came from," Anne added.

Derek looked over his shoulder. "We stick to the plan. In, grab the drop, and out. No sightseeing." They crept toward the gym doors. Derek placed a hand on the metal handle, cold and sticky. He signaled: three... two...

He yanked it open.

The gym was darker than the rest of the building, lit only by a skylight half-covered in grime. Dust motes danced in the pale light. And there, in the centre of the room.

The crate.

Bright red paint, marked with the Scottish relief symbol. Supplies. Real ones. Beside it, a flare's burned-out shell. Jennifer exhaled, a flicker of hope on her face. "Looks untouched." They moved in quickly, Anne already cutting the straps.

Callum popped the lid. Inside canned food, water purifiers, gauze, a fresh battery pack, and "Ammo," Callum said, awestruck. "Holy hell, there's ammo."

Then the sound hit them like a brick: a metallic clang from the rafters above.

They all froze.

A slow creak followed. Then the unmistakable sound of dead weight sliding on steel. Jennifer looked up and swore. A cluster of zombies, tangled in the gym's overhead scaffolding, began to fall. One by one. The dead fell right on top of them.

"AMBUSH!" Derek roared.

The first corpse hit the ground with a wet crunch, bones snapping as it writhed and lunged. Derek swung his axe mid-step, the blade splitting rotten skull. Another dropped behind him, he turned too slow. The thing grabbed his shoulder, jaws snapping inches from his face. He grunted, shoved it back

Bang! Jennifer's pistol barked, dropping it cold.

Anne screamed as a corpse slammed into her, knocking her flat. Her spear skittered away across the floor. The zombie thrashed atop her, gnashing teeth dripping foul saliva. She jammed her knee up hard, throwing it off just long enough to reach her knife. Shhk! Blade buried to the hilt. The corpse twitched and went still.

Callum fought near the crate, fists covered in blood and dirt, a crowbar in one hand, a revolver in the other. "They're everywhere!" he shouted. One zombie grabbed his coat he spun, firing point-blank. Click. Empty. He drove the crowbar into its eye socket with a yell. It dropped, and he grabbed a box of ammo from the crate, tucking it under his arm.

"Move! Out the back!" Jennifer shouted, already dragging Anne to her feet.

Derek was hacking down the last of them near the stage. His breathing was ragged, arms soaked in gore, but his eyes were sharp. "Let's go, now!"

They sprinted for the fire exit at the rear of the gym. Jennifer kicked it open, it stuck for a second, then flew wide. Cold air blasted in, along with the distant moans of more undead approaching. Derek slammed the door shut behind them, wedging a bent folding chair through the handle. They stood in an overgrown alley, panting, blood-splattered, alive.

Barely.

"Is everyone—"

"I'm fine," Anne said, wiping gore off her face.

"That was a bloody trap." Callum nodded grimly. "Zombies don't plan that. Someone put them up there."

Jennifer looked back at the building. Her voice was quiet, hard. "Which means someone was watching."

Derek glanced at the crate in Callum's arms. "Let's get back to the school. We talk after we eat."

They disappeared into the shadows, the moans of the dead trailing behind them and something else. Something watching from a rooftop above, unseen.

Chapter 2: The School

Blantyre Primary School had once been a place of learning and laughter. Now, it was steel-barred windows, fortified doors, and a perimeter of scavenged scrap rigged to maim anything that moved. It wasn't safe. But under Derek's leadership, it was still standing.

The group entered through the rear fire door as dusk spilled across the sky. Derek was the last one through, eyes sweeping the street one final time before slamming the door shut and locking it tight. His axe stayed in his hands until he was certain no one had followed.

"Liam," he said to the young lookout on guard, "get Maggie and tell her we've got a crate, food, ammo, medicine." The boy nodded and sprinted off. Liam was only 14 years old but had a sense of maturity beyond his years, he was small for his age, blonde headed. Always willing to help out whenever he could.

As Derek led the others to the library, now their command room. Maps, schedules, and rosters covered the walls. A daily log was scrawled across a blackboard. It all ran on order. On routine. On Derek. He dropped the crate on the table. Callum opened it, revealing tins of food, water purifiers, medical kits and bullets.

Anne raised an eyebrow. "This is the best drop we've seen in weeks."

"Which is exactly why I don't like it," Derek said. "It was bait. Zombies were rigged in the rafters. Somebody wanted us there."

Maggie entered, she scanned the contents, then met Derek's gaze. "You think it's a trap?"

"I know it was," he said. "They were watching. Not zombies someone with a plan."

The room went quiet. Tired eyes turned to him not out of fear, but expectation.

"What's the call then?" Jennifer asked, arms crossed, trusting him. Derek moved to the whiteboard and wrote two words in thick red marker:

"INTRUDER WATCH."

"We double shifts tonight. No fire, no lanterns after dark. I want scouts posted near the north fence. If someone's out there, we find them first."

Callum glanced at the supplies. "Still taking the food, though?"

Derek gave a rare, grim smile. "Damn right. We're not starving for someone else's game."

Anne chuckled dryly. "Now that sounds like a plan."

Maggie nodded. "We'll ration it. People need hope more than calories right now."

Later, after a quiet meal and tense inventory checks, the school settled into an uneasy stillness. The wind howled through the empty corridors. Somewhere beyond the walls, the dead wandered aimlessly. And Derek, sitting alone at the old principal's desk, stared at a hand-drawn map of Blantyre and whispered to himself "What are you planning, and when are you coming for us?"

As the others bedded down or took up their watch shifts, Jennifer climbed the stairs to the radio room once the janitor's closet, now their only line to the outside world.

As she enters the radio room, she sits at the table and slides on the headset, adjusted the frequency dial to their open-band, and pressed the mic button. Her voice was calm, practiced. "Hello... is anyone out there? This is Jennifer. We're in a safe zone. We have food, medicine, and water. If you can hear this, please respond."

The radio crackled with nothing but static.

She waited, listening to the silence.

Fifteen minutes passed. She tried again. "Hello... this is Jennifer. We're in a safe zone. We have food, medicine, and water. If you can hear this please respond. Again, static.

She repeated the call every fifteen minutes, her voice steady despite the growing sense of futility. Two hours passed. Her back ached. Her hope flickered. She reached to switch the radio off—kkktshhhh—A crackle.

Then a voice. Weak. Strained. "..Jennifer? Is that you? It's... it's Jillian."

Jennifer's breath caught. She jerked forward, grabbed the mic. "Yes! Yes, it's me. Jillian, where are you?"

Static... then—"I'm at St Joseph's Chapel. Help me... please. I'm alone. I can hardly walk..."

Jennifer's mind raced. She and Jillian hadn't seen each other since the world fell apart. She'd thought she was dead like so many others. She spoke fast, urgent. "Hold on, Jill. Stay where you are. We'll come for you." The radio hissed once more and went silent.

Jennifer didn't wait. She grabbed her coat and sprinted down the hallway, feet pounding over old tiles. She burst into the principal's office, where Derek was poring over maps. He looked up instantly. "What is it?"

"I got someone on the radio," she said, breathless. "Jillian. She's alive."

Derek stood at once, alert. "Where?"

"St Joseph's Chapel. She's hurt. Alone. She can't move far."

For a second, Derek said nothing. Then he nodded, grabbed his axe and coat. His voice was firm. "Wake Callum. Anne too. We move in ten."

Jennifer hesitated. "It could be a trap."

"It could be," Derek said. "Or it could be someone we save. Either way we're not leaving her out there."

Chapter 3: The Rescue

Callum's eyes snapped open as Derek stood over him. Anne stirred beside him, still groggy from sleep.

"We've got a situation," Derek said, voice low but urgent. He quickly explained the radio contact with Jillian alone, injured, at St Joseph's Chapel and his plan to go alone for a quick rescue.

Jennifer was waiting nearby. Her arms crossed, jaw tight. "You can't just go out there by yourself," she said sharply.

Derek met her gaze, steady. "I have to move fast. If I bring a group, it'll slow me down. If Jillian can't move far, I have to be quick." Callum wasn't having it. He stood, shaking his head.

"No way, Derek. Either I go with you, or Liam does. You don't go alone." Derek held up a hand.

"Alright. One backup. Callum, you're it." Anne sat up fully now.

"Fine, but we need a plan. And weapons." he replied.

Minutes later, the two were geared up, leaving the school in the creeping darkness. Derek led the way, axe strapped to his back, Callum carrying a shotgun. The path to the chapel stretched out like a gauntlet. The road was a war zone. Fallen barricades burned low, casting flickering shadows on piles of slow-moving zombies. The moans of the dead mixed with crackling flames and the occasional distant shout.

Halfway there, a dark shape caught their eyes, an overturned ranger's truck, abandoned and rusting. "Let's check it out," Derek said. They circled the vehicle cautiously, eyes sharp. Inside the truck bed, beneath a tarp, they discovered something unexpected: a stash of crossbows, bows, arrows, and bolts.

"Silent weapons," Callum muttered, lifting one of the crossbows carefully.

"Perfect." Derek grinned faintly. "Better than nothing." They gathered what they could carry, stuffing the weapons and some arrows into their packs. With new tools in hand, they moved onward toward the chapel, each step heavier with tension and hope. As Derek and Callum pressed forward through the darkness, the scene shifted.

Inside the crumbling walls of St Joseph's Chapel, Jillian sat huddled in a corner, bandaging a bleeding wound on her leg. Her breath came in shallow gasps, eyes flicking toward the chapel doors every few minutes as if expecting death to walk through at any moment. Her mind drifted back to how she ended up here alone and desperate.

When the apocalypse swallowed the known world, Jillian had been away with her mum and dad on holiday in St Andrews. It was the last time they'd spoken to Jennifer or Derek. "We'll come home soon," her parents had said. "And find you both." Two months passed in terrifying silence. Eventually, Jillian and her parents made it back to their house. They slipped inside, hearts pounding. But in the chaos, they hadn't noticed the shattered back window. Zombies had gotten in. As her parents went to the kitchen for supplies, they were attacked, screams, tearing flesh, and then silence. Jillian ran for the car, adrenaline driving her as she started the engine, hands shaking. She sped toward Derek and Jennifer's house, which was locked tight.

Luckily, she still had a key.

Inside, the house was eerily empty. A note sat on the kitchen table, scrawled hastily: "If you are reading this, we had to leave. Stay here. We will come for you." Jillian clung to that hope. But days stretched into weeks. Food dwindled. The silence of abandonment grew heavier. She had to leave.

The only place she trusted, the only place she could think of with supplies and shelter was the chapel.

Back in the present, Jillian wiped a tear and whispered, "Please don't let me die here." Then she heard the low, guttural moans of the dead, and frantic scratching at the chapel door. Her heart slammed in her chest. The low moans grew louder as Derek and Callum neared St Joseph's Chapel. Through the darkened windows, they spotted around twenty zombies, clustered and shuffling, scratching at the heavy wooden door.

Derek narrowed his eyes. "No way through the front."

Callum scanned the building quickly. "Side window open." Without a word, they moved silently along the stone wall. Callum found a sturdy ledge. Together, they climbed up and slipped through the cracked window into the cool, stale air of the chapel. Derek went first, crossbow raised, every muscle tense, ready for anything. Inside, silence. Just the distant groans and faint flicker of candlelight. He scanned the shadowed room.

Then he saw her, Jillian lay on a makeshift bed, pale and fragile but alive. As Derek stepped closer, Jillian suddenly jolted upright, eyes wide with fright. "Derek?" she whispered. Recognition flooded her face. Relief broke through her fear. She threw herself at him, pulling him into a fierce hug. "Thank God… you came." Jillian winced as Derek helped her to her feet, her cut on the leg bleeding but not deep. Still, she struggled to put weight on it. "I can manage," she insisted, but Derek shook his head.

"We'll take it slow. No risks." Callum moved swiftly through the chapel, flashlight sweeping over the pews and alcoves.

"No other exits," he muttered. "We may have to fight our way out."

Before Derek could respond, a loud crack echoed through the room. The heavy wooden doors buckled and burst open with a thunderous crash. The zombies poured in moaning, shambling, eyes glazed.

Derek scooped Jillian into his arms. "Callum quick, in here!"

Callum slammed the door behind them and shoved a filing cabinet against it. They were in the priest's office, small, cluttered, with faded religious icons staring down from the walls. Breathing hard, Derek looked at the barricade. The groans outside grew louder, scratching and banging on the door. "Trapped... or is this a new front line?" Callum asked grimly.

Derek's jaw tightened. "Either way, we fight."

Chapter 4: The Escape

Trapped in the cramped priest's office, Derek, Callum, and Jillian moved quickly to search for anything useful. Dusty bookshelves, old relics, and forgotten papers cluttered the room.

Callum's hand caught on something odd, a bookshelf that didn't quite sit flush against the wall. With a grunt, he pulled it aside, revealing a narrow, dark tunnel carved into the stone beneath the floor. They exchanged a tense look. It wasn't much of a choice.

Derek grabbed a couple of rags and some oil from a cracked candleholder and fashioned two makeshift torches. One for him, one for Callum. Torch in one hand, Derek carefully lifted Jillian, supporting her weight with his other arm. Together, they descended the steep stone steps into the tunnel, the air damp and cold around them. Behind them, Callum slid the bookshelf back into place and sealed the entrance with an old wooden door. With a heavy breath, he locked it tight. The groans and scratching faded as they moved deeper into the darkness. Ahead lay uncertain freedom or worse.

They reached the end of the tunnel. A heavy wooden board blocked the exit, nailed roughly in place. Derek carefully lowered Jillian to the ground. "I'll count to three. We kick it down together." Callum nodded, muscles tense. "One... two... three!"

Both slammed their boots into the boards. Wood splintered and cracked, finally giving way. They stepped out, weapons drawn, eyes scanning. The early morning light was soft but clear. They quickly got their bearings.

"We're near the shopping center," Derek said quietly, taking in the rows of closed storefronts just ahead. "About two miles from the school." Near them, an old shopping trolley sat abandoned on the cracked pavement. Derek crouched and gently lifted Jillian into it. "This'll make it easier." He handed her his crossbow, loaded and ready. "Keep this close. If anything comes, use it." Jillian nodded, gripping the weapon tightly.

The sun rose fully, spilling light over the empty streets. The rescue was far from over. The shopping trolley rattled over cracked pavement as Derek and Callum took turns pushing it along the deserted street. Jillian sat stiffly inside, clutching the crossbow, eyes darting constantly, alert for any signs of trouble. With little else to do, she scanned the surroundings, the broken windows, the abandoned cars, and the occasional distant groan that reminded them the dead were never far behind.

Every so often, they stopped. While one pushed, the other moved carefully through nearby houses and shops, scavenging what supplies they could, bottled water, canned food, anything useful. Evening was fast approaching and as they passed a battered house with curtains drawn, Derek spotted movement at the window.

"Wait," he whispered.

They both froze as two figures appeared, waving hesitantly. Jillian waved back weakly, a flicker of hope sparking in her tired eyes. Moments later, the door creaked open, and the strangers stepped outside, cautious but friendly. A woman stepped forward, her eyes wary but kind.

"Hi, I'm Ellie. This is my husband, Daryl, and our son, Zak."

Derek smiled and nodded, introducing himself, Callum, and Jillian. Then he asked, "How long have you been here? How many of you?"

"Just the three of us," Ellie replied. "This is our home. When the announcement came to stay indoors, we did. But my husband ran one of those stores nearby. He went back, took all the stock he had, and brought it here. We've got enough food to last us a year." She glanced behind her at the sturdy door, worn but intact. "The zombies have been getting worse, moving in hordes, trying to get in. But the doors have held."

Derek considered this, then offered, "We have a base not far from here. We're building a community there. You and your family are welcome to join us."

Ellie looked at Daryl and Zak, then nodded. "We'd like that. But night is approaching, if use are happy to, we can all stay here and then head out in the morning."

Derek, Callum and Jillian discussed it amongst themselves and all agreed.

"Ok" Derek replies, "we accept your offer, in the morning, we can leave together."

Ellie hurries them in and bolts the doors shuts

They gathered as much food, water, and supplies that they could carry, ready to move with Derek's group. The group now numbering 6 headed to the school with new found Friends.

Chapter 5: The Return

It had been two long days since Derek and Callum left to find Jillian. Jennifer and Anne grew increasingly restless, the silence dragging heavy. They were only meant to be gone for a day at most. Fear settled deep in their bones. Jennifer and Anne huddled together in the dim light, trying to comfort one another, sharing whispered hopes that the others were safe. As dawn broke on the sixth day, a sudden pounding on the roof startled them both.

Liam came running down the ladder from the lookout post, breathless. "People approaching. At least six of them. They look armed." Everyone scrambled up to the roof. Jennifer grabbed her binoculars, heart pounding. She focused on the distant figures moving toward the school. Jennifer's eyes widened as the figures drew closer through the morning haze.

"It's them!" she cried out.

Without hesitation, everyone rushed down to the main doors and out to the perimeter fence. Derek's group pulled up, dust rising from the trolley wheels. Jennifer ran forward and threw her arms around Jillian, holding her tight in a long, relieved hug. She stepped back briefly, took the trolley from Derek, and kissed him quickly on the cheek before leading Jillian inside. Anne grabbed Callum's arm, smiling wide.

"What no kiss?" he joked.

Anne shot him a sharp look. She turns to the newcomers. "Who are they?"

Ellie stepped forward, smiling warmly. "I'm Ellie, this is my husband Daryl, and this young man is our son Zak." They all moved inside, the gate and main door closing firmly behind them. Inside the safety of the base, introductions were made, and the small group began to settle, the weight of the outside world momentarily held at bay.

Jennifer pulled Jillian aside, her voice soft but steady. "Tell me what happened to our parents. And how did you end up at the chapel?"

Jillian swallowed hard, eyes distant. "Before the outbreak we were on holiday in St Andrews as you know. We were told to stay put in our lodge and not leave, but mum and dad wanted to get home to get us all together. When we came back, our house was ransacked, the back window smashed. Zombies got in and attacked mum and dad while they were in the kitchen looking for supplies. I ran, drove to your house... but use never came back. I stayed until the food ran out, then had no choice but to leave. The only place I thought to go was the chapel, it had food stores and felt like the only safe place." Jennifer nodded, holding her sister's hand. "You're safe now."

Meanwhile, the rest of the group gathered, making introductions with Ellie, Daryl, and Zak. Derek and Daryl gravitated towards each other, deep in conversation. "So, tell me more about yourself Daryl, Derek asked.

Daryl smiled. "I'm a keen hunter and tracker. I know how to hunt, skin animals, and live off the land."

Derek studied him as he spoke—tall, about six-one, with a mop of brown hair that never seemed to sit right. The man never stopped scanning the room, eyes flicking from door to window as if he expected trouble to come crashing through at any moment.

Jennifer finally emerged, seeking out Ellie for a quieter conversation. "I want to get to know you better," Jennifer said gently.

Jillian sat nearby, safely looked after by Maggie, who had quickly taken a protective shine to her.

The group was stronger now united in hope and survival.

Chapter 6: A New Normal

Life inside the school had slowly begun to shift. The return of Derek, Callum, and Jillian had lifted a heavy weight off everyone's shoulders. With Ellie, Daryl, and young Zak joining them, the halls no longer felt so empty.

Within days, the newcomers integrated with surprising ease. Ellie took over ration management with Jennifer, while Daryl began showing the others how to track and hunt. Zak became a beacon of light in the group, making the older survivors smile with his curiosity and jokes. Together, they expanded their safe zone within the school. The old science block was turned into living quarters. The nurse's office became a proper infirmary. Hallways were cleared, classrooms organized into usable spaces. At night, they gathered in the library, sharing stories by candlelight.

As the school transformed into something like a home, so did the people inside it.

Jillian was finally walking on her own again. Her leg still ached in the mornings, but the worst had passed. With the pain fading, her focus turned to something else: the people who had risked their lives to save her. She found Callum out by the barricades, hammer in hand, sweat on his brow. "Hey," she called softly.

He looked up and smiled. "Back on your feet, huh?"

"Thanks to you," she said. "I mean it. You didn't have to come."

Callum shrugged, glancing away. "Yeah, well... Derek wasn't going without someone watching his back. I just... did what needed doing."

"You risked everything," Jillian said. "That's not nothing."

He gave her a crooked smile. "Just don't go running into a chapel full of zombies again, all right?" She laughed and turned to go, the heaviness in her chest lighter than before.

Later that day, Jillian found Derek alone in the old art room, hunched over a map, planning patrol routes. "Got a minute?" she asked from the doorway.

He looked up and nodded. "Yeah. Come in."

She stepped inside, her voice gentle. "I never got to say thank you. For saving me. For carrying me. For everything." Derek met her eyes.

"You're my family. That's what we do." She walked over and wrapped her arms around him. He froze for a moment, then returned the hug.

"I wouldn't be here if it weren't for you," she said softly.

"You're here," he replied. "That's what matters." She smiled through glassy eyes.

"And I'm ready to help now. However I can."

Derek nodded. "Good. We'll need everyone."

Outside, the sun dipped low as voices carried through the corridors, laughter mixing with the occasional barked command. Within those walls, people weren't just surviving anymore they were living. The school had begun to take on a rhythm, mornings were for chores and patrols, afternoons for training or repairs, and evenings for quiet moments, sharing meals and memories.

Jennifer had stepped fully into her role as caretaker and coordinator. Every morning, she walked the halls with a clipboard, checking in with each group, ensuring no one was falling behind on their duties or spirits. She had a calm presence, but those who knew her best could sense the weight on her shoulders. She often found herself up late, alone in the old computer lab they now used for planning. She'd stare at maps and notes, lists of supplies and shifts, always thinking five steps ahead. But when she wasn't organizing, she'd sit with Jillian and Ellie, laughing gently, letting herself feel like a sister again instead of just a leader.

One quiet night, as Jillian dozed beside her, Jennifer whispered, "I thought I'd lost you. I don't think I would've come back from that."

Jillian stirred, her voice sleepy but sure. "You didn't lose me. Not even close." They sat there in silence, the kind only shared between people who've seen the worst and survived it.

Callum had become the unspoken glue of the group. He never sought attention, but he was always there when needed, shoring up barricades, checking traps with Daryl, or even patching up leaks in the ceiling with Liam. He and Anne had grown closer too. Their banter had become routine, their shared laughter a welcome sound echoing through empty classrooms. But behind the humor was a man haunted by close calls.

He often checked on Jillian without saying much, just a nod or a brief smile. She knew he carried the weight of responsibility, even if he didn't show it. One afternoon, as he sharpened a blade out by the courtyard, Jillian sat beside him.

"You don't talk much," she said.

Callum smirked. "Talking's overrated."

She nudged him gently. "Still. I appreciate you. And I think you're one of the good ones."

He glanced at her, that familiar lopsided grin on his face. "I'll take that."

Daryl had become indispensable. His hunting trips were yielding fresh meat, squirrel, rabbit, even a couple of pheasants. But it was his calm, methodical way that really won people over. He taught Liam and Zak how to track animals, and how to listen to the woods. His stories, often told in a low voice by firelight, became something the group looked forward to. Despite his quiet nature, he and Derek had formed a fast bond. They often worked together on patrol routes, sharing hunting tips or strategies for expanding the perimeter. One evening, Derek and Daryl were talking.

"Think there's more to be found out there?" Derek asked.

"Food, maybe. The forest is full of game, but something else too. That feeling you get when something's watching you. We're not the only ones adapting." It was a chilling thought but one that made Derek respect him all the more.

Jillian, now stronger on her feet, had taken up assisting Ellie in the kitchen and sorting supplies. She wasn't a fighter, not yet but she had a sharp mind and a fierce determination to pull her weight. She often walked with Zak around the halls, keeping him busy and cheerful. When not helping with chores, she'd talk with Jennifer or read old books in the library. But behind the calm, her eyes still held strong memories of her parents, the chapel, the days alone. Yet each day, she grew more confident, more present. At night, she sometimes found herself looking out the old windows toward the woods, gripping the crossbow Derek had given her.

She thought back to the trip home with her parents, how scared she was as her dad drove. Cars and vans littered the roads. Some overturned, some on fire, it was chaos. The drive home took a lot longer than it should have. Swerving in and out of cars, trying to avoid contact with anyone whatsoever. She was absolutely terrified.

"I'm not running again," she whispered to herself one night. "Next time... I'll be ready."

Chapter 7: The Stranger

The sky was bleeding into night, the last golden hues swallowed by clouds. Daryl stood on the rooftop of the school, crossbow in hand, eyes scanning the quiet horizon. It had been a peaceful day, too peaceful.

Then he saw it. A lone figure walking slowly up the cracked pavement toward the front gate. Daryl stiffened. He stepped to the edge of the roof and raised his binoculars. The figure wore a long, black leather trench coat, the hood pulled over their head. No visible weapons. No pack. No vehicle. Just... walking.

He didn't like it.

Slamming the butt of the crossbow twice against the rooftop railing, he sounded the alarm two sharp thuds, a signal they'd all come to recognize. Within moments, Derek, Jennifer, and Callum appeared from different parts of the school grounds and climbed quickly to the roof. Daryl pointed. "He's been walking straight at us for the last five minutes. Not one glance to the sides. That's not someone looking for shelter. That's someone who knows where they're going."
The four of them moved to the front edge of the roof, weapons at the ready, as the man came to a slow stop at the main gate.

He looked up at them, silent for a long moment. Then he raised both hands peacefully, and in a voice clear and calm said, "I've been watching you."

No one moved.

The stranger reached up slowly and pushed back his hood. He was in his late 40s, with short-cropped dark hair streaked with grey, eyes sharp and calculating. "I saw you at the community centre," he said, voice steady. "I watched you at the chapel. My name is Ellis. I'm the leader of a community called New Kinross." The name meant nothing to them.

He continued, "We have over forty people, families, fighters, engineers. We're organized. And we're looking for other survivors. You've built something here. We should talk. Come down to the gate."

Derek's eyes narrowed. "He's alone," he muttered.

Callum nodded, tensing. "No pack. No car. Where's he been living, the trees?"

Jennifer frowned. "What kind of leader shows up without even one escort?"

Daryl shifted his grip on the crossbow. "Something about this stinks."

Derek didn't take his eyes off Ellis. His instincts had kept them alive this long, and right now, they were screaming. "Let's see what he has to say," he said finally, voice low. "But we keep that gate shut."

The four leaders Derek, Jennifer, Callum, and Daryl moved cautiously through the school's reinforced corridor and out to the front gate. Derek led the way, every step purposeful, his hand resting on the handle of his machete. Jennifer's rifle was slung but ready.

Callum held a baseball bat wrapped in wire, and Daryl's crossbow remained aimed low but loaded.

Ellis stood calm, hands still visible, just beyond the fence. Up close, he looked like a man who had once worn authority well. His coat was worn but clean, boots polished, his presence too deliberate. He wasn't desperate. He was calculating. Derek stepped forward. "You said your name is Ellis. You've been watching us?"

Ellis nodded, his expression friendly but unreadable. "Only out of caution. I've seen too many dangerous groups to take chances. But from what I observed... you're different. Organized. Disciplined. Survivors."

Jennifer crossed her arms. "You've been spying on us."

Ellis gave a small smile. "Scouting. I didn't approach until I was sure you weren't cannibals or raiders."

"And now you're sure?" Daryl asked, voice gruff.

"I am," Ellis said. "And I think we can help each other." Callum glanced at Derek, who gave a slight nod.

"We're listening," Derek said.

Ellis straightened, clasping his hands in front of him. "New Kinross is about half a day's walk northeast. We have real infrastructure, solar power, greenhouses, security. But what we don't have enough of is leadership. Fighters. People like you." He made eye contact with each of them in turn, his voice calm and practiced. "You've built something good here. But how long can you hold it? The dead are growing in numbers. Supplies will run dry. Bandits are becoming bolder. You know that as well as I do. Join us. Bring your people. You'll be protected. Valued."

Jennifer's expression didn't change. "And what do you get out of it?"

Ellis chuckled lightly. "Strong allies. A fortified location. A leader like Derek on my council. People like Callum and Daryl keeping the perimeter safe. I've read enough to know you're not fools. I'm offering you a future."

Derek stepped a little closer to the gate, eyes narrowing. "You came alone. No map. No food. No proof this place even exists. You expect us to trust your word?"

Ellis didn't flinch. "I expect you to think long-term. What you've done here it's impressive. But it won't last forever. With us, it could. I came alone because I didn't want to threaten you. I'm here with an olive branch."

"Or bait," Daryl muttered under his breath.

Ellis tilted his head slightly, catching it. "You're right to be cautious. I would be too. But if I wanted to harm you... I've had chances. I chose not to. That has to count for something." A long silence followed. The wind picked up, rustling the tall grass. Finally,

Derek spoke, cold and firm. "We'll think about it."

Ellis gave a small bow of his head. "That's all I ask."

"Now turn around," Derek added. "And walk back the way you came. If we want to talk again, we'll find you."

Ellis lingered for a heartbeat longer, then nodded. "I'll be waiting." He pulled up his hood and turned, walking off into the fading light with the same measured pace he arrived with.

Once he was gone, Callum muttered, "Smooth talker. Knows exactly what to say."

"But not why," Jennifer said, brows furrowed.

Daryl still watched the path. "He's hiding something. That wasn't an introduction... It was a test."

Derek's jaw tightened. "And now we know one thing for sure: someone's been watching us longer than we thought. And we need to figure out what Ellis really wants."

Ellis moved with practiced ease through the decaying streets, his trench coat sweeping behind him like a shadow. Once the school was out of sight, his expression shifted no longer polite or composed, but cold, meticulous. The mask he wore at the gate had served its purpose. Now, he was back in control. He ducked into an abandoned petrol station, drew a military-grade radio from an inside pocket, and pressed the call button twice.

A voice crackled through. "Go ahead."

"I made contact," Ellis said. "They're skeptical. But curious. Suspicion's good means they're careful, not paranoid. They'll listen again."

"Did they ask about numbers?"

"Of course," Ellis said. "I told them we had a dozen, maybe a few more." He glanced northeast, where faint orange glows from watchfires marked the distant silhouette of New Kinross." They don't know the truth."

Behind that silhouette stood a fortress, a walled compound of reinforced concrete and salvaged steel. Once a housing estate, Ellis had transformed it into a thriving, militarized community of over two hundred people. Massive walls ten feet high ringed the perimeter, topped with scrap metal spikes and floodlights. The front gates, reinforced with shipping container doors, could withstand an armoured truck. There were guards posted every fifty feet, snipers, patrolmen, and lookouts with night-vision scopes. Inside, makeshift barracks, storage bunkers, and a central command post thrived. Fields grew food. Workshops built weapons. Below it all, in the darkened basement of a former community hall, a different kind of operation continued, one that involved labs, locked cages, and screams no one ever spoke of again.

Ellis lit a cigarette and took a long drag.

"They've got supplies. Water. Security," he said into the radio. "But more than that they've got hope. That makes people follow."

The voice on the other end was sharp now. "What's the plan?"

"Same as always. Gain trust. Create dependence. Then offer safety.. at a cost."

"And if they refuse?"

Ellis flicked the cigarette to the ground and crushed it beneath his boot. "Then we take what we want." He turned toward the northeast road, his coat flaring in the wind. "New Kinross will expand. Whether they like it or not." Behind him, the silence of the dead city watched and waited.

Chapter 8: New Kinross

The metal gates of New Kinross groaned open as Ellis approached, a figure of authority in his black trench coat, hood now pulled down. Spotlights flared across the perimeter wall, tracking his every step. Guards on the high catwalks snapped salutes, rifles slung across their backs, eyes sharp.

At the gate, Bellamy stood waiting, tall and lean, his silver-streaked hair pulled tight in a knot. The military fatigues were no surprise; he wore them like a second skin. Early forties, steady as stone, he was Ellis's right hand, the one who handled the work no one else wanted to admit was being done."You made contact," Bellamy said flatly.

Ellis nodded. "They're cautious but intrigued. They'll bite."

Bellamy smirked. "Good. Dr. Mirak says he wants to see you, it's urgent, Subject Twelve is stabilizing, I was told to tell you".

Ellis's lips curled slightly. "About time." They passed under the archway into New Kinross, a compound unlike anything left in the central belt of Scotland. Inside the towering walls, the community buzzed with organized purpose. People moved in squads, some patrolling, some repairing, some farming in tight plots of land carved between the rows of reinforced homes. Children ran quietly between designated play zones, all under the watchful eyes of armed guards. It was safe here, secure.. but it was no paradise. Every home had a curfew. Every adult wore an identification band. Every entrance and exit was logged. Cameras salvaged from shopping centers and banks watched from every corner. Those who disobeyed vanished. And no one asked questions.

Ellis walked toward the central command tower, a retrofitted apartment block reinforced with sheet metal and lookout points. But instead of heading to the top, he entered through a side entrance and descended. Below the tower, through a coded metal door and down two more flights of stairs, the air grew cold and sterile. Fluorescent lights buzzed above him as he stepped into a hidden corridor lined with biohazard warnings.

At the end: the Lab.

Inside, white-coated figures moved between computers, specimen tanks, and reinforced cells. A low growl echoed from behind one of the sealed doors, something not quite human anymore.

"Subject Twelve nearly turned last night," said Dr. Mirak, wiping blood from his gloves. He was in his early 50's Caucasian. Little hair and was terrified of Ellis "But the new compound dose slowed it."

"We're getting closer," Ellis said, approaching the glass tank where a humanoid figure writhed in agony. "We're going to control this plague. Not just survive it, own it." Ellis's eyes never left the twitching, snarling figure in the tank.

Above them, life in New Kinross went on disciplined, loyal, blind. Below, in the dark, the real work continued. And soon, the world would remember the name Ellis.

Ellis stood before the reinforced glass of the observation chamber, his arms folded, face unreadable. Inside, Subject Twelve once a man, now something far removed, twitched in sporadic spasms. Its eyes were milky white, its mouth sewn with crude surgical wire to prevent it from biting, though it still tried. Behind him, Dr. Mirak approached, clipboard in hand, flanked by two other white-coated figures Dr. Ngoba, a geneticist, and Dr. Leith, a neurologist with a past that had been thoroughly scrubbed from any surviving database.

"It's responding to the compound," Mirak began. "The neural inhibitors we injected last week have reduced its aggression during light stimulus tests."

Ellis turned, one brow raised. "Reduced... but not eliminated."

"No. But we're getting closer," Dr. Leith chimed in, tapping a chart on her tablet. "We ran a response trial using strobe-light cues. Subject Twelve paused movement for nearly six seconds after each signal."

Ellis paced slowly, hands clasped behind his back. "That's not obedience. That's hesitation."

"We're not dealing with trained dogs," Mirak replied. "Their brain function is... fractured. The virus rewires the frontal cortex, and basic motor function remains, but decision-making is chaotic."

"Then remove chaos," Ellis snapped. "I don't need a soldier that twitches at lights. I want one that halts on command, attacks on order, and spares who I say to spare."

Dr. Ngoba cleared her throat. "We've started neural mapping from surviving test samples. We think we can isolate the reaction triggers. But..."

Ellis turned to face her fully. "But?" he asked, voice low and dangerous.

"We need more test subjects," she said carefully. "Fresh ones. Recently turned. The decay in the current batch is corrupting our results."

Ellis nodded slowly. "You'll get what you need. Prepare the equipment." He turned back to the glass, watching Subject Twelve slump against the wall in a half-lucid state. "Once I can command them," Ellis said under his breath, "I won't need to convince anyone. Not the school. Not the others out there hiding behind fences. We'll build an army that never sleeps, never stops."

"And then?" Mirak asked.

Ellis's eyes narrowed. "Then I take back the world."

Behind the glass, Subject Twelve lifted its head slowly, its blind eyes staring through the reinforced wall at its creator, its master in waiting. Above the labs, the world felt almost peaceful.

In the open courtyard at the heart of Kinross, families gathered under makeshift awnings and solar lamps.

Children played with scavenged toys. A small group practiced guitar near the fire pit, old songs echoing off concrete walls. To the uninformed, it could have been mistaken for a rural village untouched by the apocalypse. Mira, a schoolteacher in her late twenties, stood in front of a chalkboard nailed to a wall, surrounded by half a dozen young children. She smiled as they sounded out words written in crumbling chalk: hope, shelter, survive. The children laughed when one misspoke, a rare joy these days. Mira's heart ached knowing how precious and temporary moments like these were.

Near the farming plots, Marcus, a lanky man with sun-creased skin and strong hands, showed a teenager how to adjust a solar irrigation line. "See this?" he said, pointing. "We save more water this way. Everything counts. That's how we stay alive."

Across the community, routine ruled. Citizens reported for their work details at dawn, logged their hours with Bellamy's officers, and returned to their homes by curfew. Lights dimmed at 8:30pm sharp. Patrols rotated every four hours. Infractions though rare were quietly corrected. They all knew Ellis kept them safe. They all believed in Kinross. But what they didn't know, what none of them could know was the true cost of their safety.

No one questioned the small groups that disappeared during lockdowns. No one asked why the infirmary was guarded or why injured newcomers were sometimes "relocated" and never seen again. The official answer was always the same: "They didn't make it." The truth lived below ground, masked in clinical language and white lights. Test subjects. Viral controls. Obedience trials.

And Ellis liked it that way.

That night, as the courtyard dimmed and people retreated behind their bolted doors, a soft humming filled the air. Power rerouted from the solar grid surged downward to the labs, to the restraints, to the observation rooms where the real work never stopped.

Above, a child whispered a bedtime prayer to the moon.

Below, Subject Thirteen opened its eyes for the first time.

Chapter 9: Suspicion

The wind had picked up outside the school. Clouds rolled in, painting the sky in greys and hints of storm. Inside the former staff room turned meeting hall, tension hung in the air like static before a lightning strike. Derek sat at the head of the old conference table, elbows on the scarred wood, brow furrowed in thought. Jennifer leaned next to him, arms crossed, her eyes distant but alert. Callum slouched in a chair with his boot propped up, rolling a screwdriver between his fingers. Jillian sat quietly, her eyes darting between everyone. Daryl, still dust-covered from his tracking run, stood with his hands on the back of a chair.

"No backup. No vehicle. And now this," Derek muttered, glancing at Daryl. "Tell them exactly what you saw."

Daryl nodded, his voice low and steady. "I followed him. Two miles, easy. He never once looked behind him. No scouting, no caution. Just walked like he owned the road. Lit a cigarette around the old petrol station, turned a corner... and gone. Like that." Callum raised an eyebrow. "Gone? No trace?" "I swept the whole area twice. No tracks, no smell. It's like he vanished."

"That's not right," Jennifer said. "You don't last long out there walking like that unless you're either crazy or... protected."

Jillian spoke up, her voice soft but firm. "Or it's a trap. He knew someone would follow him."

"Exactly," Derek said, tapping the table with two fingers. "He said what we wanted to hear. Safe walls, food, scientists. But it was rehearsed. Controlled. And now this disappearing act?"

Callum leaned forward. "I don't like it. That man gives me the creeps. Something about his eyes cold, dead. Like he's seen too much and doesn't care anymore."

Jennifer looked to Derek. "What do you think?"

"I think Ellis is hiding something. And I think that something has teeth," Derek said. "He came here alone to size us up. To see how we run, who we protect, how strong our defences are. You don't do that unless you're planning something."

Daryl crossed his arms. "You want me to try again? Head out tonight, pick up a fresh trail?"

"No," Derek shook his head. "He wanted us to follow him. I won't play that game again. From now on, we stay alert. Increase perimeter patrols. Rotate the watch more often."

"And what if he comes back?" Jillian asked.

Derek's expression hardened. "Then this time, we tell him to hit the highroad and go back under the rock he crawled out from.

The school buzzed with quiet urgency. What was once a cold, silent shell of a building had become a hive of movement. The smell of sawdust and old metal filled the air as everyone sprang into action. Ellis's appearance had shaken them but it had also galvanized them. Derek's scavenging team was first out. He moved with practiced efficiency, his crossbow slung over his back, eyes scanning every street corner. Jillian walked beside him, gripping a short blade, trying to hide her nerves behind a determined face. Jennifer had been hesitant to let her go, but Jillian had insisted.

"I have to do something," she'd said. "I can't sit around anymore. I won't."

Jennifer had pulled her close before they left. "Stay with Derek. Don't do anything stupid. You're my family."

As they crept through the remains of a nearby industrial estate, Jillian stuck close. Derek glanced at her often, checking her footing, watching her back. They found a partially looted medical warehouse with some supplies still intact under debris. Bandages, iodine, painkillers. Everything mattered now. Jillian even managed a small smile as she helped pull a crate of canned food from under a collapsed shelf.

"You're doing great," Derek said, giving her a nod. She stood taller.

Callum's group wasn't far behind him, Daryl, and Liam headed east toward an old hunting shop. With Daryl's experience and Liam's energy, they worked like a tight unit, retrieving supplies that could reinforce the perimeter: thick netting, barbed wire, even a roll of fencing still sealed in its plastic. The more they gathered, the better their odds.

Back at the school, Jennifer had taken command. She moved from room to room, sleeves rolled up, sweat glistening at her brow. The others followed her lead without question. They tore apart the upper floors, stripping away desks, doors, lockers, anything solid that could be repurposed. Anne and Maggie fashioned barricades with reinforced hinges, bolting them to the ground-floor windows. Shaun and Harry nailed down panels across weak points in the halls. The building creaked under the effort, but with every new layer of protection, it felt more like a fortress.

Still, Jennifer's thoughts kept drifting. Every time she heard a noise outside, her stomach twisted. Jillian was out there again. Out there with the dead, and with whatever Ellis truly was. She caught a glimpse of her reflection in a shattered whiteboard, her face streaked with dust, lips pressed into a hard line. She turned away, clenching her fists. They would not be caught off guard again. She shouted instructions across the hall, her voice firm. "Make sure all ground-level doors are double-barred. I want two people stationed at every entry point at all times. If anything even moves out there we're ready."

From the rooftop, Harry radioed down. "Jennifer, the perimeter's clear for now."

"Good," she said. "But stay sharp. We don't know what's coming."

Outside, the sky began to darken. Somewhere, far off, a distant screech echoed over the city. And at the school, the survivors dug in.

Derek knelt beside a crate of drill bits, brushing dust from the packaging. "Jackpot," he muttered with a grin. Timber, nails, hinges, saws, even a stack of power tools with fully charged batteries. It was as if time had stopped in the hardware store when the world ended. A goldmine for rebuilding, and they had it all to themselves. Jillian entered from the front, arms filled with thick rope, tarpaulin, and a handful of hand tools. She dropped them beside the growing pile near the loading bay.

"There's a truck in the garage," she said. "Still got fuel that smells old, but might be enough." Derek moved quickly, sliding the garage door open and inspecting the vehicle. A delivery truck, small enough to be maneuverable, large enough to haul half the store.

"Let's get loading," he said, tossing a crowbar to Jillian. They worked fast. But just as Derek hoisted a box of nails onto the truck bed, something caught his attention, a flicker of movement in the far shadows of the garage. He froze, his hand drifting to the crossbow slung over his shoulder.

"Come out," he said firmly, aiming into the gloom. "I saw you."

A tense moment passed. Then a figure stepped forward slowly, hands half-raised. He looked rough late twenties, beard scruff, dirt covering most of his face, eyes alert. In one hand, a baseball bat. "Drop it," Derek barked.

The man hesitated, then obeyed, letting the bat clatter to the concrete floor. Jillian had entered behind Derek and instinctively ducked behind him, blade in hand. He stared at them, then squinted. "Derek? Derek Anderson?"

Derek blinked. "Lee?" A grin broke across the stranger's face. "Holy hell, it is you." Derek lowered the crossbow. "Lee, you son of a bitch... I nearly put a bolt through your eye." The two embraced briefly, laughter and disbelief mingling in the moment. Lee was an old friend of Derek's, 29 with fuzzy black hair. Well built around 5ft 9. Jillian watched carefully, still tense. "I thought you were dead," Derek said. "What are you doing here? Who are you with?"

Lee motioned them to follow. "Come on. I'll show you." He led them through the back of the store, past shelves and storage rooms, until they reached a heavy metal door hidden behind a set of broken shelves. He pushed it open, revealing a narrow staircase that descended into darkness.

Derek hesitated.

"It's safe," Lee said. "I promise."

They descended. At the bottom, a single flickering LED light illuminated a large basement room rows of shelving had been cleared to make space. Cots and blankets lay scattered around. Crates of food, bottled water, and supplies were stacked against the walls.

Roughly fifteen people, men, women, even two children sat or moved about quietly.

A woman in her forties looked up. "Everything all right, Lee?"

"Yeah. Just... an old friend." Derek and Jillian looked around in disbelief. These people were surviving in silence, hidden away beneath a hardware store, only blocks from routes they'd scavenged a dozen times.

Lee led Derek to a makeshift bench in the corner. They sat. "I've been here since the first month," Lee said. "When it all fell apart, I was in the store. People came looking for supplies I helped where I could. Some stayed. We blocked the stairwell, scavenged at night. Been hiding ever since."

"You kept them all alive," Derek said, impressed.

"Barely. Food's running low now. Water too. We've been lucky." He paused. "What about you?"

Derek gave him a general overview and talked about the school, the group, their scavenging, the fences. He told Lee about Ellis too, about the mysterious leader and the fortified Kinross. But he kept their base location vague. Trust was earned these days.

"I don't like the sound of that guy," Lee muttered. "Anyone showing up alone and talking like that? Not right."

Derek nodded. "That's what we think too."

As Lee stepped away to check on one of the older men, Jillian leaned in close to Derek and whispered,

"Should we ask them to come with us… back to the school? They're not going to last down here forever."

Derek looked around the dim basement. Tired faces. Thin bodies. Quiet suffering. It was no way to live, and if they stayed, they'd eventually run out of everything: supplies, hope, life. He gave a slow nod. "Yes… let's put it to them," he said quietly. "But we explain the dangers first. We're not promising safety, we're promising a fight. The road back won't be easy, and if Ellis or anyone else comes looking, they'll be part of our war too."

Jillian nodded.

Derek stood, raising his voice just enough to gather attention without causing alarm. "Lee," he called, "can we talk to everyone?" Lee looked puzzled but waved everyone over. One by one, they gathered around their footsteps soft on the concrete, their eyes cautious but curious. Derek stepped forward, Jillian by his side. "We've got a place," he said, voice firm. "It's secure, reinforced, and it's home to good people. We grow food, we've got clean water, and we defend ourselves."

A murmur passed through the group.

"But it's not perfect," Derek added. "We're under constant threat. The dead are always close. And now… there's a man named Ellis, from a community called Kinross. We don't trust him. We think there's more to him than he's telling us. So if you come with us, you're not just joining a home. You're joining a fight." He paused. "No one will force you. But if you're willing… we'll bring you with us. We'll protect each other." The room fell quiet. For a few moments, all you could hear was the low hum of the LED light and the distant wind rattling through the building above.

Then an older man stepped forward. "Better to fight with others than starve alone." A few heads nodded.

A young woman hugged her child closer and whispered, "We'll come."

Lee met Derek's gaze. "Looks like we're in."

Derek let out a quiet breath and gave a small nod. "Then we leave at dawn. Let's load that truck with everything we can."

Jennifer stood by the classroom window, arms folded tightly, watching the horizon. It was getting late. No word yet from Derek's group or Callum's. She sighed and turned back to the main hall where Anne, Maggie, and Shaun were sorting through a new batch of supplies from an earlier run. The school was changing. They had reinforced nearly all ground-level windows and doors with timber, metal, and anything salvageable. The classrooms were converted into dormitories, storage, and even a small medical area. Children laughed quietly in the upstairs halls while a few adults tended the rooftop garden harvested vegetables now a rare but welcome sight.

Jennifer had taken to walking the perimeter several times a day, clipboard in hand, mapping vulnerabilities, listing what was needed. Her mind was constantly buzzing with worry not just for Derek and Jillian, but for the whole group. She was leading while he was gone, and the weight of that role was beginning to wear on her.

Callum, Daryl, and Liam crouched low behind a row of abandoned cars in a crumbling car park. Across from them stood a small community pharmacy mostly intact. Daryl peeked through binoculars, then muttered,

"No movement. No zombies. But... it's too quiet." Callum motioned them forward.

They reached the door quickly and quietly. Liam popped the lock with a tool kit while Daryl kept watch. Inside, the shelves had been picked over, but the back storage room yielded results: painkillers, antibiotics, gauze, even insulin.

"Jackpot," Liam said, stuffing a bag. Callum grabbed another medical crate and glanced out the back window. His eyes narrowed.

"Movement."

Daryl followed his line of sight. Four figures, slow-moving. zombies. "No big deal," Daryl said. But they weren't alone. A scream echoed from deeper in the block. A human scream.

Callum swore under his breath. "We don't have time—"

"I'm not leaving anyone behind," Liam said.

Daryl already had his weapon up. "If someone's alive, we can't just walk away."

Callum hesitated but only for a moment. "Grab what we can and move. Fast."

Callum motioned for silence as they crept around the pharmacy's back wall, the muffled scream still echoing faintly. The alley was tight and cluttered with bins, smashed crates, and the stench of rot. Daryl moved first, crossbow raised, while Liam kept low with a crowbar ready in hand. They reached the source, an old corner laundrette, door hanging off the hinge. The scream came again, weaker this time.

Inside, a woman was backed into a corner, swinging a broken mop handle wildly at a slow-moving zombie. Another zombie was tangled in laundry cords near the door, arms flailing uselessly. Callum didn't hesitate. He shoved past the door, grabbed the zombie from behind and drove his knife through its skull. Daryl finished the second one, bolt clean through the eye. The woman collapsed in relief, gasping.

"Harper?" Liam asked, kneeling next to her.

She looked up, eyes wide with disbelief. "Liam? Oh my god. I thought you were dead."

"Likewise."

Callum stepped forward, eyes scanning the building. "Anyone else with you?"

Harper hesitated. "Yes, two others. We're holed up across the street in the old locksmith's. They're injured. Bad. I came out for help... didn't think I'd make it."

"We need to move," Daryl said, already looking back toward the pharmacy. "We can come back for supplies later."

Callum nodded. "Alright. Liam, help Harper. Daryl, cover us."

They darted across the street, entering the locksmith's. Inside, two figures lay under makeshift blankets, an older man clutching his leg, badly bandaged, and a young girl barely conscious. Supplies were low. Hope even lower.

Callum knelt beside them, checking their wounds. "We'll get you somewhere safe."

Harper touched his arm. "Are you with a group? Would they take us in?"

He nodded. "We are. But we have to move now. Can you walk?"

The man groaned. "Not fast."

"We'll carry you," Daryl said firmly. "Let's go." They strapped a plank to a trolley from the laundrette and used it to wheel the injured man. The girl was carried by Liam, with Harper helping steady her. Callum led the way, Daryl watching the rear. As they moved out, Callum kept his hand on his blade. His instincts were humming. If they ran into a pack, they were done. But his thoughts were on something else now how many other survivors were still out there, barely holding on? And more urgently... How many could they take in before it broke them?

The gates of the school were just coming into view as the sun dipped low, casting long shadows across the car park. Jennifer and Maggie stood by the main entrance, gear packed, ready to leave on their own scouting mission when movement caught Jennifer's eye. She raised her binoculars. "It's Callum!" she shouted. "They're back!" They both sprinted to the perimeter fence. As Callum's group approached, Jennifer immediately noticed the extra people, the makeshift stretcher being wheeled, the girl clutched in Liam's arms, and Harper helping Daryl carry the old man.

Jennifer rushed forward. "What happened? Who are they?"

Callum gave her a tired look, brushing dust off his arms. "Survivors. Found them holed up near the old laundrette. One's got a busted leg. The girl's weak dehydrated."

"Is Derek back?" he asked.

Jennifer shook her head, her eyes dimming. "Not yet. He and Jillian haven't radioed either. We were just about to head out and find them."

Callum frowned. "One more day. If they're not back by then, we go."

Jennifer nodded solemnly. "Deal." Maggie quickly took charge, directing Liam and Harper toward the medical bay. The older man groaned as he was lifted from the trolley and onto a stretcher inside. The young girl was laid gently beside him, Maggie already checking her pulse. Jennifer lingered by the doors as the sky darkened, glancing down the long road beyond the fence.

Where was Derek? Are they safe?

Chapter 10: The Return

Morning broke over the grey skyline, casting pale light across the silent streets. Derek had been awake since 3 a.m., sitting on an overturned crate beside the truck. Jillian sat next to him, both keeping watch while the others prepared to move out.

They'd been talking for hours, their conversation drifting from the harsh reality of the present to memories of the world that once was lazy Sundays, laughter over coffee, old music that used to play in the background of better days.

"I still remember your beat-up old car," Jillian said, managing a small smile. "The one that always stalled at traffic lights."

Derek chuckled. "yeah that thing was falling apart, but it was mine and I loved my wee nova."

Around 8 a.m., Lee emerged from the basement and approached them, the wear of the apocalypse showing in the lines on his face. He gave Derek a nod. "We're packed and ready."

It took some effort, but they managed to load all fifteen people into the truck. Supplies were crammed into every available space. The engine roared to life just enough fuel left to get them back to the school, if luck held.

As they pulled out, Derek gripped the wheel tightly. His eyes scanned the roads ahead, but his mind was on Kinross. What did Ellis want? When would he return and with who?

Meanwhile, at the school, Callum was on lookout duty when he spotted the dust trail in the distance. He grabbed the binoculars and zeroed in. "Truck approaching looks full. Everyone to your stations!" Jennifer and Maggie were about to leave the building to start a fresh reinforcement job when the alarm went off. Maggie snatched the binoculars and squinted. Then she smiled.

"Weapons down it's Derek!"

Cheers rippled through the group as the school gates opened. Jennifer and Callum were already moving when the truck pulled in and stopped.

Derek climbed out first, tired but smiling. "Got supplies and company." Jennifer rushed to him and wrapped her arms around him tightly, then turned to help Jillian down from the truck.

Callum glanced past them at the group unloading. "All this... from one store?"

Derek shook his head. "No. An old friend of mine, Lee, had people holed up in the hardware store basement. They needed help."

As the newcomers stepped inside the perimeter, Jennifer ran over and hugged Lee, she hadn't seen him for nearly 3 years. She told him they would catch up when things settled down.

The two injured newcomers were quickly taken to the school's makeshift medical bay. Supplies were sorted, food rationed, and introductions made. The group was growing, and so were the challenges but for a moment, they had a win. A hard-fought one.

The calm before the next storm.

Lee's group had been shown around the school grounds shortly after their arrival. There were clear rules, some areas open, others strictly off limits, mostly for safety and resource reasons. The gym, now a food storage space. The old science wing turned into a med bay. And the upper floors are still being reinforced, marked as private quarters or restricted zones.

The newcomers were grateful, tired, and quiet, slowly filtering into their assigned spaces. Some helped unload supplies; others helped cook. It would take time for full trust to form, but so far, things were calm.

Later that evening, the core group gathered in what used to be the teachers' lounge. The table was scratched and worn, but it had become the command centre, the beating heart of their little society. Derek sat at the head, flanked by familiar and new faces: Callum, Daryl, Jennifer, Jillian, Maggie, and now Lee.

"Alright," Derek began, resting his arms on the table. "First order of business we need a signal." He glanced around the room. "If someone's coming back to base, especially from a run, we need a way to let the lookout know it's us. We don't want anyone getting shot for just walking up to the gate." He let out a small, dry laugh, but his eyes were serious.

Maggie nodded. "Agreed. Maybe a whistle pattern? Three short, two long?"

"Simple's best," Daryl added.

"We'll test a few options." Derek leaned forward. "Second thing this group here," he gestured around the table, "you're the council. We all have a say in how this place runs. No one person should bear it all."

Daryl raised his eyebrows and smirked. "Sure, but let's not pretend. Derek's still the man in charge."

The others murmured agreement. Derek just nodded, slightly uncomfortable.

"If you're all sure..." he muttered. Derek didn't like being the man in charge, he preferred to follow orders rather than give them.

Jennifer gave him a firm look. "We are."

"Third," Derek continued, his voice darkening. "Ellis. We know he's coming back. And I don't trust a man who walks two miles, never once looks over his shoulder, and then disappears into thin air."

Jillian leaned in, visibly tense. "You think he's watching us?"

"I know he is," Daryl muttered. "I tracked him, remember? He was l too smooth. Too confident. He wanted to be seen."

Derek nodded. "I want drills. Combat training for anyone who can hold a weapon. Rotation schedules for patrols. Supplies moved to secure areas. We can't be caught off guard."

Callum cleared his throat. "And the fourth thing is a backup plan." The group turned to him. "We need a fallback position," he said. "If we're overrun, if Kinross makes a move, whatever it is we need somewhere to go. A plan, pre-packed gear, exit strategy. This school is good, but it's not invincible."

There was a moment of silence, the weight of their situation hanging heavy in the air.

"Alright," Derek said finally. "We break into teams tomorrow. Callum, Daryl you scout possible fallback sites. Maggie, work with Lee and the new folks on training. Jennifer, coordinates defenses and patrols. Jillian, you and I will work on supply checks and escape kits." Everyone nodded.

Lee leaned back slightly, glancing around the table. "You've built something solid here," he said. "I'm honored to be part of it."

Derek looked at him carefully. "You've got a place here now, Lee. But everyone pulls their weight. Let the others we brought in know this too."

Lee nodded. And with that, the meeting broke, plans forming, pressure rising. The calm was over. The storm was coming.

Life at the school was starting to settle into something that could be classed as normal. Although the school now resembled a fortified building. The world outside was in chaos, zombies controlled the world now, it was theirs but inside, people were talking, forming friendships, children playing, people felt safe, at least for now.

Chapter 11 – Kinross and Subject 13

Life inside Kinross moved with a strange rhythm disciplined, structured, but tense beneath the surface. Concrete walls rose high above, hiding the chaos of the outside world. Patrols marched regularly through the narrow streets, boots echoing across cracked tarmac. Armed men and women checked IDs, stood at barricades, and watched from towers. Children played, but only in marked safe zones, always under watch. The community was run like a fortress… because it was one.

Bellamy stood in his office, a small room on the second-last floor of the old tower block that overlooked the entire camp. From his window, he observed the world below civilians farming in the courtyard, guards running drills, engineers repairing fences. To the people of Kinross, Bellamy was the iron fist; Ellis, the shadowed mind behind it all.

Ellis entered quietly, his long black trench coat trailing behind him. "I leave in two days," he told Bellamy without ceremony. "I'll be heading to the school again alone."

Bellamy turned, frowning. "You sure about that?"

"I am," Ellis replied. "It's time Derek gave me his answer." He smirked, voice dipping lower. "I should be back no later than five days. Be ready to either move out.. or welcome our new guests." His smirk widened into a cold, calculated laugh.

Bellamy didn't laugh.

Later that evening, Ellis descended into the hidden depths of Kinross. The air grew colder as he passed through reinforced doors and entered the restricted zone. Fluorescent lights buzzed overhead, casting a sterile white glow on steel walls and reinforced glass enclosures. At the center of it all was Dr. Mirak, lead scientist of the Kinross initiative. Mirak looked up from a tablet, his eyes sunken from lack of sleep.

"Sir," he greeted. "I have something... promising to show you."

They walked past cages and sealed rooms, arriving at one large glass chamber. Inside stood Subject 13 an undead figure stripped of its former identity, dressed in restraints, a collar laced with electrodes around its neck. Mirak raised a hand. "Watch." Through a microphone he gave commands:

"Walk."

Subject 13 shuffled forward.

"Stop."

It halted.

"Turn around."

It obeyed with a slow, jerking motion.

"Bite."

It lunged at the glass violently, teeth snapping.

Ellis's grin widened.

But as a technician approached too close to the chamber wall, Subject 13 slammed itself against the glass and cracked it. The tech screamed and stumbled back, terrified. "He still attacks instinctively if people get too close," Mirak admitted, clearly frustrated. "They're not fully stable. They're.. responsive, but unpredictable."

Ellis clapped slowly, eyes gleaming.

"They are ready."

"Sir" Mirak tried to protest.

"How many?" Ellis asked sharply.

"Twelve Subject 13 prototypes. All showing varying levels of command compliance. But I strongly advise against deployment. Not yet." Ellis turned to him, eyes cold and merciless.

"Doctor, we don't wait for perfection. We build with chaos. When I return, prepare them." He looked back at Subject 13, who stared at him through the glass, unmoving.

"A new kind of army," Ellis whispered. "And they'll never see it coming."

Ellis was up before dawn, the air still thick with dew as he dressed in his signature black leather trench coat. The mines outside Kinross loomed in the distance, quiet and untouched for weeks. He called

Bellamy to his side in the command building. "I want two cages set up," Ellis said calmly, not looking up from his map. "Position them near the entrance to the mines, under cover. Leave them alone. No questions."

Bellamy raised an eyebrow, the corner of his mouth twitching. "Cages, sir?"

Ellis looked up slowly. "Covered. Forgotten." A silent beat passed before Bellamy nodded.

"Understood."

As he left the room, Bellamy muttered to himself, "He's eccentric... but smart." Still, a strange weight settled in his gut.

Later that morning, Ellis strode confidently through Kinross. His steps echoed off stone walls. He didn't glance back. He didn't look around corners. He moved like a man who couldn't be touched. "Open the gates," he ordered. Bellamy stood at the lookout tower above the main gate, watching Ellis vanish into the wild, a lone figure swallowed by the horizon. Then he turned to his men.

"You heard him. Get those cages ready. Covered. Leave them by the mine. No one goes near them." He scanned the camp. "Every fighter, be combat ready. Five days."

Below, Kinross moved into action, unaware of what was coming.

Ellis's walk was not direct. He took strategic detours. Watching. Studying. He lingered in ruined towns and monitored clusters of undead from a distance, muttering notes to himself, sometimes scribbling in a notebook. Some he approached, giving short sharp whistle tones, watching their reactions. He noted their gait, their alertness, their speed. This was his fieldwork.

What should have been a half-day journey took two full days.

Preparations had been relentless.

Callum and Daryl had departed on recon three days earlier with strict instructions to survey escape routes, identify fallback points, and return in three days. No contact unless urgent. Inside the school, the core group held strong.

Maggie and Lee had taken charge of weapons training. Arrows thudded against makeshift targets all day. Lee's experience in stealth and quick strikes made him a natural instructor, while Maggie's quiet steadiness inspired confidence.

Jennifer had emerged as the school's second commander while Callum wasn't here, coordinating patrols, restructuring defences, organizing the daily routine with almost military efficiency. She had become a tactician, respected and relied upon. Derek and Jillian were stationed in one of the classrooms-turned-supply-rooms. Packs were laid out across the floor. Jillian knelt beside him, handing him water bottles and bandages. Each pack had food, water, bandages, and a knife.

"We'll split into six groups," Derek explained. "Five adults and one or two kids per group. Each team gets two packs." He looked up at Jillian. "We don't run unless we have to. But if we do, we do it smart."

"Do you really think it'll come to that?" she asked.

"I don't want to think that," he replied, "but we have to be ready."

As the sun began to dip low, Jennifer entered the room. Derek didn't notice her at first, still packing. She walked straight up to him, wrapped her arms around his neck, and kissed him slowly, full of longing. Derek responded, holding her waist. Jillian turned her head away, busying herself with folding a jacket. But a flicker of something crossed her face. Jealousy, quiet and unspoken.

Three days had passed. Daryl and Callum had returned mere hours ago, battered but alive, and were reporting back to Derek.

Suddenly, a voice thundered from outside the perimeter.

"DEREK! I'M HERE!"

The group froze. Everyone turned.

Jennifer rushed to the lookout.

There he stood. Alone again. Ellis. Megaphone in hand. Hood pulled back. Smiling.

"Weapons up," Derek ordered quietly.

"No," Jennifer said, "we need to hear him out first."

Derek nodded grimly. "But keep everyone ready."

Chapter 12 – The Mission (3 days earlier)

Callum adjusted the straps of his rucksack as he and
Daryl set off at first light. The wind carried a chill, but
the skies were clear. Their boots crunched over
broken tarmac as they moved west away from the
school, and more importantly, away from Kinross.
The mission was simple: find potential fallback
locations. They had three days.

By nightfall on Day One, they had covered miles of
ground staying off the main roads, moving through
forests and along dried-up streambeds. They stopped
to rest in the remains of a crumbled petrol station,
taking shifts through the night, neither really could
sleep. Instead they spoke about life before the fall.

Callum told him how he was the best man at his
wedding. He shared stories of the things they used to
get upto. Like when they used to play chappy as kids,
and there was always this one house that you done
but had to leg it as the guy used to chase you,
sometimes got hours on end.

Both sniggered.

Daryl told him all about himself as well, how he was
passed about foster homes as a kid. His troubles with
the police when he was younger, till he met Ellie, she
grounded him, made him grow up. Into the man he
was now.

Day Two was all about scouting. They approached every site with caution, weapons always raised, eyes sweeping for movement.

The first site they marked was an abandoned primary school small, one-story, and half-covered in vines. It had no outer wall or fence, but the structure seemed sturdy and had potential for fortification. Next was an apartment block surrounded by a chain-link fence. The building itself was intact, and a few hastily made barricades suggested someone had tried to hold out there once. Signs of struggle were evident but no bodies. Daryl made a mark on the map.

Then came a prison grim and foreboding. Towering grey walls and rusted fences, with guard towers still standing. It would be a fortress if they could clear it, but the risk was high. They noted it as a last resort.

Late in the afternoon, as the sun began to dip, Daryl spotted something. "Callum," he said, pointing, "Bus depot."Dozens of buses sat in rows behind a long wire fence. A few wrecks lay near the front, burnt out, but the back lot looked untouched.

"Could be something," Callum said, squinting through binoculars.

"Not just something," Daryl replied. "If even one of those buses works, we can move everyone at once. No splitting up."

They found a small tear in the perimeter fencing and slipped through quietly. The air inside was thick with dust and rust. Weeds had grown tall between the rows of buses, some of which still had intact windows. A few had doors ajar. Birds had nested inside one. Weapons raised, they moved cautiously between the parked vehicles, checking each one. Callum opened the door to a workshop garage inside were spare parts, tires, even a dusty toolbox on the workbench. He grinned.

Daryl walked over to a large yellow school bus and pushed open the driver's door. He climbed inside, checking the dashboard. "No keys," he muttered, then checked under the visor. Nothing.

Then Callum called out, "Found an office! Might be something useful inside."

They regrouped at the admin office near the back of the depot. The door was partially jammed but gave way with a hard shove. Inside, old paperwork littered the floor, along with a corkboard map of the city and a set of labelled keys hanging on hooks. Daryl grabbed a bundle marked "Lot 3 - Back Row."

"Jackpot," he said with a grin.

They didn't start the engines too risky to make noise. Instead, they used the remaining daylight to sweep the area, securing all entry points and taking notes. One bus in the back even had a half-full fuel tank, according to the gauge. They camped that night on top of two buses, taking turns to keep watch. The depot felt promising but they wouldn't count it safe until it had been thoroughly secured.

In the morning, they'd make their way back to the school with news that might change everything. With the sun creeping over the rooftops of the city, casting an amber glow on the weathered buses, Callum stood beside one of the larger models, a full-sized transport with decent clearance and intact tires. "Let's see if she still breathes," he said, giving Daryl a glance. Together, they quietly pushed the bus down a slight incline toward a workshop garage directly in front of them. The rusted door creaked open just enough to fit the vehicle, and once inside, Daryl climbed behind the wheel while Callum crouched by the engine bay, eyes darting around.

"Moment of truth," Daryl muttered. He turned the key they'd found in the admin office. The engine coughed once, twice, and then roared to life with a deep rumble. A cloud of smoke belched from the rear.

Callum grinned, clapping the side of the bus. "Looks good." "Plenty of fuel too.

But let's not push our luck," Daryl said, quickly killing the engine. The silence that followed was deafening.

Callum checked his watch. "Six hours till we have to move. Let's make the most of it." They split up, scavenging across the depot like men on a mission. Every drawer, cupboard, and locker was searched. Every bus was cracked open. The undead were few, mostly drivers or passengers who'd turned early. Those they found, they dealt with swiftly and quietly.

One garage had a half-collapsed roof, but inside, they found shelves of spare parts, belts, hoses, tools, wrenches, screwdrivers, pliers, oil cans. Callum packed everything into crates and dragged them to the bus. In a back office, Daryl discovered a stash of

15-litre water bottles, likely intended for the old water dispensers. The seals were unbroken. He grabbed as many as he could carry and returned to the bus.

By midmorning, the bus was filling fast. Medical supplies, old uniforms they could use for extra clothes, even a few battery packs that might still hold charge. Callum even found a toolkit for changing tires, neatly stored under a hidden floorboard in one of the minibuses. They were just about to make their final round when the sound of a car engine reached their ears.

Daryl froze mid-step. "You hear that?"

Both dropped low behind a stacked row of tires and watched as a dark sedan pulled up to the depot gate. The vehicle paused, then a man stepped out, unlocked the gate with a key, and drove in. He made his way to the far side of the lot, stopping at a second garage, then disappeared inside.

"Not one of ours," Callum whispered, his hand tightening on his weapon. "We wait,"

Daryl replied. "If he sees the bus has been moved, this could get messy."

Minutes turned into an hour. Then two. Eventually, the garage door opened again. The man walked back to the sedan, started the engine, and calmly drove off, locking the gate behind him like nothing had happened. The moment the car vanishes down the road, Daryl stood. "We're gone."

They moved fast, throwing the last of the supplies into the bus. Callum lifted the side shutter of the garage, eyes scanning the horizon. The coast was clear. With the sun now fully risen on the third day, Callum started the engine again. It came to life with a growl. Daryl took up position near the front with his rifle ready as they pulled out of the depot. They didn't stop. Taking back roads and alleyways, the bus rumbled toward the school. It was a long, tense journey, and they kept eyes on every rooftop and corner, but nothing followed them. The city remained silent.

When they reached the school grounds, they entered from the north side, hiding the bus behind the tech building, under cover of trees and shadow. They would unload it later. Daryl let out a breath as he stepped off the bus. "Just in time."

Inside, the others had already heard the rumble of the engine. Jennifer and Maggie were at the north stairwell within moments, relief washing over their faces.

"You made it," Jennifer said, her eyes darting past Callum to the bus.

"Yeah," Callum nodded, his expression serious. "And we've got a ride."

The mission was complete but something about that lone driver at the depot lingered in both their minds. Something was coming.

And it had already begun.

Ellis stood just beyond the main gate, clad once again in his long black trench coat, the hood pulled back to reveal his ever-composed, unreadable face. The undead wandered lazily in the distance behind him, but none dared approach him. He didn't flinch, didn't even spare them a glance. He stood tall, still, confident unnaturally so. From the rooftop,

Daryl watched him through the scope of his crossbow. "He's alone. Again. Just like last time."

Derek, Jennifer, Callum, Jillian, Daryl, and Lee descended to the lower level and exited through the reinforced hallway that led to the inner gate. Maggie flanked them from behind, crossbow in hand. Everyone was on edge. Derek stepped forward, hands at his sides but tension in every inch of his posture. "Ellis," he said simply.

Ellis's pale eyes flicked to each of them in turn, and a thin smile tugged at the corners of his mouth. "I see you've been busy," Ellis said, glancing up at the new barricades, the posted guards, and the higher walls made from salvaged metal and desks. "Impressive improvements. You've done well."

"Get to it," Callum muttered, not bothering to hide his irritation.

Ellis's eyes didn't leave Derek's. "I'll come to the reason I'm here."

He paused, letting silence stretch, testing their patience. "I gave you time, Derek. Time to consider the benefits of an alliance. But alliances, like opportunities, have a shelf life. I'm here to ask again, will you join us at Kinross? The offer still stands."

Derek narrowed his eyes. "And what exactly are you offering? You still haven't said what you really want."

Ellis gave a small, almost amused chuckle. "Safety. Security. A future. Kinross is strong, fortified, self-sustaining. Together, our communities could rebuild something greater. And I assure you, we have resources you don't."

Jennifer crossed her arms. "Then why not bring proof of that? Why come alone again?"

"Because I'm not here to intimidate," Ellis replied calmly. "I'm here to speak leader to leader. I left the soldiers and banners behind on purpose. What we build together must start with trust."

"Hard to trust someone who vanishes into thin air after lighting a smoke," Daryl said flatly.

Ellis turned his head toward Daryl slowly. "You followed me. I expected as much."

Derek stepped forward slightly. "You said you'd give us time. We've used it. And we've prepared. We don't take decisions like this lightly. If we move or ally with the wrong people, it costs lives. I need more than words."

Ellis's smile faded. His expression grew neutral, professional. "I understand. That's why I'm staying nearby for two nights, no more. Think on it. I won't wait forever." He turned to leave but paused. "Oh and if you decide not to come with me, I'd recommend staying very, very ready." With that, he began to walk away, not even glancing back.

The group stood there in silence for a moment before Derek turned to the others. "Let's double the watch. I want every exit prepped, every weapon checked. He's not just scouting. He's planning."

Callum nodded grimly. "And so are we."

Chapter 13 – No Turning Back

The leadership group sat in the school's main office, the table now marked and worn from constant planning, maps, and stress. Derek stood at the head, arms crossed, his expression hard. "We're all agreed," he said. "We're not joining Ellis."

Heads nodded around the table Callum, Jennifer, Daryl, Jillian, Maggie, and Lee. No one argued. The last visit had only confirmed their worst fears. Ellis wasn't interested in unity. He wanted control. "But that means we need a plan," Derek continued. "Because he's coming. And not for another talk."

They all looked at the map laid out in front of them. Circled locations, arrows, fallback routes. A single bus now symbolized their lifeline.

Daryl leaned forward. "We need more fuel. That bus won't make it far if we're not ready." "I'll go," he said. "Take Lee and Shaun with me."

Derek looked him in the eye. "Six hours. No more."

The three men left swiftly, knowing time was now the enemy. While they were gone, the others got to work on the bus. They reinforced the frame, welding scrap metal to its sides and front. Bars were fitted to all windows and the windshield, thick enough to keep out the undead but spaced just wide enough to see through. Small slits were cut into the walls at head height meant for blades, spears, anything that could be thrust out to defend the bus as it moved.

Jennifer oversaw the modifications, barking orders and adjusting plans. "Don't weld that too high, we'll need to see from the inside."

Jillian and Maggie packed the remaining supplies into plastic containers, loading them carefully into the luggage compartments underneath. Dried food, water, medical supplies, anything they had spare that might be going with them. The rest would be left to live off.

As dusk neared, the fuel team returned. They took the truck Derek had brought back earlier with Lee's group, inside were half a dozen full jerry cans and several plastic bottles filled with fuel. They funneled every drop into the bus and stored the rest in the back.

Lee did a quick calculation. "Should be enough to get us two hundred forty, maybe fifty miles if we're careful." It wasn't much, but it was enough for now.

Two days had passed.

Everyone in the school could feel it, that sense of time running out. Weapons were distributed. Escape bags prepped and stashed near the bus. Even the kids were briefed, given small packs and paired with adults. Each group had a role, a plan, a direction. Just in case they couldn't make it to the bus.

Then, like the shift in wind before a storm, he returned.

Ellis.

The lookouts called it in. Derek and the leadership team were already heading for the gate. Ellis stood alone once again. But this time, something in his stance had changed, no more charm, no patience, no riddles.

"Last chance, Derek," he called, his voice sharp and cold. "What's your answer?"

Derek stepped forward, calm and unmoved. "You already know the answer," he said. "Turn around and go back under the rock you crawled out of."

Ellis's lips curled into a smile, small, satisfied. "I hoped you'd say that." He turned on his heel, and as he began walking away, he raised his hand lazily and spoke a single word over his shoulder.

"Soon."

He didn't look back.

Derek looked around at the others. "Everyone ready. This is it." There was no turning back now.

Back at Kinross. It had been five long days since Ellis had departed. Bellamy stood on the ramparts, just after 9 a.m, watching the horizon with a gnawing unease in his chest. The sentries had reported no signs of movement, but he had a feeling today would be different.

And it was.

A lone figure appeared on the road, calm, steady, unfazed. It was Ellis. Bellamy exhaled, but the unease didn't fade. He was alone.

Two days before Ellis returned. It was still dark when Bellamy began his rounds, just past 3 a.m. He moved along the south-west perimeter when something caught his eye, a blinking light near the old railway line, beyond the compound's edge. Suspicious but cautious, he grabbed his rifle and quietly slipped out of Kinross. The night was cold, the silence oppressive. He reached the rail line where the light had flashed.

Then, movement.

Five men emerged from the shadows, their weapons visible but lowered. Bellamy raised his gun instinctively.

"No need for that, Bellamy," one of them said coolly.

"How do you know my name?" Bellamy demanded.

 A sixth figure stepped from behind a wrecked van, older than the others, his eyes sharp. "My name is Couper," he said. "These are my associates. We used to work with Ellis, long before the world fell apart." Bellamy's expression hardened.

"Ellis never mentioned you."

"He wouldn't," Couper replied. "Not after what happened."

He went on to explain how, after the outbreak, they'd formed a tight-knit community. Ellis had a wife and two kids. They had a good thing going, until a horde overran their camp. Ellis lost everything that day. "Something broke in him," Couper said. "He became obsessed with controlling the undead. Said he'd never lose anyone again, not if he could control them."

Bellamy scoffed at the idea, but Couper wasn't finished. "You've heard of Dr. Mirak?"

Bellamy nodded slowly.

"He's down there in the mines, beneath your feet, building something terrible. We've got a man inside. He told us about the experiments. About the.. cages. Ellis tried this before at his last compound in Kintyre. It failed badly. The undead swarmed the base. Now he's trying again. And this time, he won't stop." Bellamy's face tightened as Couper placed a hand on his shoulder. "You seem like a good man. Be careful. Ellis doesn't need loyalty, he needs obedience." And just like that, they vanished into the night.

Bellamy stood there, stunned, until a flashlight suddenly snapped on him.

"Who's there?" a voice called.

"It's me, Bellamy. I thought I saw something. All clear," he had lied.

"Copy that."

Ellis sat in his office after he got back, gazing out the window as Bellamy entered.

"The army's ready, sir," Bellamy said.

Ellis didn't turn. "We leave in two hours. But first.. I need you to come with me." Bellamy followed him down into the underground research facility, where the hum of generators and the eerie silence of sterile rooms made his skin crawl.

Dr. Mirak stood waiting. "Sir, the ZF 13s are loaded in their transport cages and ready, except one."

Ellis raised an eyebrow. "Why not all of them?" Mirak led them to an observation room, where a large reinforced glass pane showed a young woman locked inside a cell. Across from her, one of the subject 13 trials paced slowly, its skin gray, eyes dulled but focused.

"She stole from the kitchen," Mirak said coldly. "A good test."

They watched.

"Sit," Mirak said firmly into the mic. The zombie sat.

" Attack," he added.

The zombie tried to get to the woman through the cage.

"STOP" Mirak ordered. The zombie stopped and went back to pacing.

"She's been in there twelve hours," Mirak explained. "No aggression.."

Ellis smiled. "Brilliant."

Bellamy's stomach churned.

Ellis turned. "We only need twenty fighters. Have the rest stand down." Bellamy nodded stiffly.

Two Hours Later

A small convoy prepared to leave Kinross. Ellis. Bellamy. Twenty handpicked soldiers. And two trucks hauling the mysterious cages.

Only Ellis and Bellamy knew what was inside them. As the convoy rolled out, Bellamy looked back one last time, a storm brewing in his gut. He now knew the truth. Ellis wasn't leading a mission of peace or survival. He was leading a crusade of control, and monsters.

Chapter 14 – The War at the School

Derek stood outside the garage, watching everyone move like a well-oiled machine. Every person, regardless of age, had a job and took it seriously. Even the kids pitched in, grinning, laughing, and turning the loading process into a contest: who could carry the most without dropping anything. Old Bill stood by the bus with a watchful eye, shotgun across his chest and a determined glare that said he wasn't about to let anything happen to the young ones. Inside the meeting room, Derek took a breath. The silence was brief.

Jennifer walked in first, her eyes tired but filled with affection. She stepped up to him, wrapped her arms around his neck, and kissed him slowly, deliberately. When they pulled apart, she gave him a firm look. "You got this." Before Derek could respond, Callum barged in.

"Hey Derek," he said with a grin, "I hope you're not expecting a kiss from me too."

Derek snorted. "Only if you close your eyes."

Callum laughed. "Bus is loaded. Kids are on board with Old Bill. He's itching for action. Says he's still got one good eye and both good shots."

Jennifer rolled her eyes. Bill was all scars and grit, grey-bearded and half-blind, but no one doubted his aim or his resolve. She smacked Callum's shoulder as she left the room.

Next came Jillian. She hesitated by the doorway, watching Jennifer and Callum exit. Her eyes lingered for a moment longer than necessary. Then she stepped inside.

"I've done all I can," she said quietly.

Derek looked up and nodded. "I know."

She shifted uncomfortably, rubbing her hands together. "I'm scared. Trying not to show it, but... I don't know if I can hold it together."

Derek stood and placed a hand on her shoulder. "We're all scared, Jill. But right now, we've got to bury it deep. Get through today. Then we feel it." She nodded, eyes glassy. He pulled her into a hug, strong and protective. She held on tightly, not wanting to let go.

"Thanks for taking care of me," she whispered.

"You're family," Derek said, pressing a gentle kiss to the top of her head. "I'll always take care of you."

Just then—The alarm rang.

A sharp, shrill wail that echoed across the school grounds. People froze for a heartbeat... and then snapped into motion. Callum's voice crackled over the radio. "Ellis. He's back. And he's not alone."

Derek rushed outside.

From the north lookout, Maggie called out with the binoculars. "We've got vehicles. Two trucks. Maybe twenty men. And... oh god... cages. Two of them."

"Zombies?" Callum asked, appearing beside her with his rifle.

"Not sure, they are covered." "Get everyone to their posts," Derek said. The courtyard became a flurry of motion. People ran to windows and walls, grabbing weapons. Crossbows loaded, rifles chambered, knives handed out. Jennifer directed defenders along the front barricade, shouting quick orders. Lee and Shaun checked the fallback positions.

On the roof, Daryl took position with his scoped crossbow. "If he makes a move, I've got him."

The gates stood closed and locked. Derek stood in the center, staring down the road. Ellis stood on the far end of the street, arms folded, his twisted grin already waiting for him. Behind him: twenty armed soldiers.

And behind them…

Two heavy cages covered with tarps. The breeze lifted one of the corners. And inside, something shifted. Something… wrong.

"Time's up, Derek!" Ellis shouted through a megaphone. "Last offer was already made. This is your consequence."

Derek gritted his teeth. "No turning back now," he muttered. And the battle for the school was about to begin.

Two groups.

Two leaders.

Two futures.

Derek stood firm at the main gates, crossbow drawn, finger resting lightly on the trigger. His eyes never left Ellis, who stood across the battlefield, smug and confident. The tension in the air crackled like a live wire.

"WEAPONS READY!" Ellis barked, his voice thundering through the megaphone. "TAKE—"

Thwip.

A crossbow bolt whizzed past his face, slicing his cheek open before embedding itself into the eye socket of the man behind him. The fighter collapsed without a sound. Ellis staggered back in surprise, hand to his face. His eyes burned with rage. "OPEN FIRE!" A hailstorm of bullets roared across the field, tearing into the barricades and walls of the school. The windows shattered. Sandbags burst. Chunks of wood and brick exploded under the relentless volley. Derek's group returned fire, calculated, measured. They conserved their precious ammunition, hitting targets when they had clear shots. Callum and Lee coordinated the defenders, yelling positions and targets through the chaos. Then Ellis's next move, a small team rushed forward, attaching ropes from the gate to a truck parked behind cover.

"FULL REVERSE!"

The truck roared to life. Chains pulled taut. The creaking of stressed metal screamed before BOOM the gates burst outwards, splinters flying. Ellis's group surged forward. Derek's people retreated inside the school. The clash had cost them five already. Ellis had lost at least ten, but he still had his trump card. His ZF-13s... untouched. Ellis's remaining fighters, only 10 remaining, rushed to the main entrance, trying to rope it like the gate. But Derek's group was waiting on the first floor. From above, they opened fire, crossbows and guns ripping through the enemy. Four more of Ellis's fighters dropped.

"FALL BACK!" Ellis roared.

He stepped forward alone and pulled a heavy launcher from his back. He knelt, aimed at the school's grand front door.

Derek's eyes widened. "EVERYONE TAKE COVER!"

BOOM!

The explosion was deafening. The world shook as the entrance was obliterated into burning rubble. Smoke and fire poured through the corridor.

"IS EVERYONE OK?" Derek yelled, coughing, ears ringing.

"I'm fine!" "Still here!"

"We're good!" came replies, then a scream.

"MY LEGS! I CAN'T FEEL MY LEGS!" It was Lily. Derek looked and saw the horror, her lower half pinned beneath a collapsed beam. Blood soaked the floor. She was crying in agony. Shaun and Zak... didn't respond. Their bodies were broken, too close to the blast. Gone. Then came the next horror.

"Bring them in!" Ellis commanded.

The truck reversed up. Bellamy jumped out, still pale from what he'd seen in the labs. The cage covers were pulled away. Everyone inside the school froze. There they were. The ZF-13s. Twelve zombies, eyes hollow, bodies twitching. Standing upright. Still. Waiting. Ellis opened the cages and pointed. "Go. Kill them all." They shuffled forward, mechanically. Two turned back. One snarled at Ellis, the other lunged.

BANG-BANG!

Bellamy didn't hesitate. He put both down. The rest entered the school, like unleashed nightmares. Screams followed. A man tried to run. Bitten. A woman stabbed one in the neck, it didn't even flinch.

"FALL BACK!" Derek screamed.

What was left of his group, sixteen now, retreated toward the bus. The entrance behind them filled with the groans of the dead. Fire. Blood. Smoke. Ellis stood outside, watching. Laughing. Until a low rumble stole his joy. The ground quaked slightly. Dust lifted in the breeze. A noise, a chorus of moans and snarls. From the east. From the woods.

Bellamy turned. "Horde," he said, pale-faced. Ellis stopped laughing.

"MOVE! MOVE NOW!"

They scrambled. Bellamy shoved Ellis into the truck, jumped in beside him. The remaining fighters raced to their vehicles. The ZF-13s were still inside the school, devouring and clawing anything that moved. The horde poured into the school as the convoy disappeared down the road, unseen by Derek's people. At the bus, the surviving group clambered aboard. Lily was pulled on, her screams fading into shocked silence. Ross slammed the doors shut.

But—

"Where's Jillian?!" Jennifer yelled, eyes scanning the courtyard. "DEREK!" she screamed, turning to him, but he was gone.

"I'LL FIND HER!" his voice echoed back. "GET THE BUS OUT!"

"Derek, NO!" Jennifer screams.

He turned back, silenced pistol in hand, and looked at them one last time. "We meet at the other school. GO!" The bus engine roared to life. Dust kicked up. Doors slammed. And they were gone.

The fire. The dead. The ruin.

Ellis believed he'd won. But Derek was still alive. And he wasn't finished yet.

Chapter 15 – Ghosts in the Halls

Smoke still lingered in the air, curling up through the shattered remains of the school's entrance as Derek crept down the corridor, pistol drawn, steps light. Below him, the bottom floor teemed with death. The horde, dozens of them, moved in a slow, disjointed rhythm, groaning softly like they'd forgotten why they were there. The blast had stunned more than just Derek's group. Dust and debris blanketed the floor, muffling even the undead's steps. But they weren't what haunted him most. It was the six ZF-13s that stood frozen amidst the chaos. Unlike the others, they weren't aimless. They scanned. They listened. They were hunting. Derek pressed his back against a scorched wall, heart pounding. He peered down the corridor and saw one of them twitch, just slightly, like a machine booting up. He couldn't let them get out. He wouldn't. Silencer on, he crept forward and took them down, one by one. Clean, calculated shots to the head. They barely made a sound as they fell, collapsing like puppets with their strings cut. But one was different.

Smarter. It had watched.

When the fifth went down, the last ZF-13 suddenly turned and disappeared into a room, out of sight. Derek's eyes narrowed. He stepped forward, tension in every muscle. He reached the doorframe and saw only darkness. He reached into his bag, pulled out a makeshift grenade, glass bottle, nails, and a shortened fuse. Strike. Toss. Turn.

BOOM!

The shockwave ripped the doorframe, throwing body parts across the hall. Derek waited, breathing hard. He stepped over the threshold, scanning the room. Nothing moved. He didn't know if he got it. But if it was still out there, it wasn't showing itself.

He turned and moved. Level 1 was scorched and quiet. He searched every room he could, calling for Jillian in a low voice. Nothing. No signs. Only the distant groans below. Then… something caught his eye. In the foyer, dangling from the shattered skylight above, the corner of a torn green shirt.

Jillian's shirt.

Of course. She's on the roof. He rushed to the emergency exit stairwell, it had been twisted by the blast, but the rope-ladder they'd rigged weeks ago during drills still hung from the broken rafters. Hand over hand, he climbed. At the top, beyond the broken hatch, he found her, curled behind a barricade of metal sheets and sandbags, shaking.

"Jillian!" he called, voice low but urgent. "It's me, it's Derek!"

Her head snapped up. The moment she saw him, she ran, throwing herself into his arms, trembling. "I was so scared," she whispered, holding onto him like she might fall through the roof. "I saw the explosion… I was already up here and… and I saw the bus leave, I thought you all left me behind." She pulled back, tears in her eyes. "Thank you," she said. Then, before he could speak, she kissed him. A deep, desperate kiss.

One filled with fear, relief... and something else. But just as fast, she pulled away, eyes wide. "I, I'm sorry, Derek. That was stupid. I didn't mean to—"

Derek, caught off guard but calm, placed a hand on her shoulder. "It's okay," he said gently. "You've been through hell. Don't apologize." She looked down, nodding, trying to hide her flushed face. "Right," Derek said, switching gears. "Here's the plan." He crouched beside her and laid it out. "The garage is on the ground floor. There's a truck still in there, we can use it to get to the fallback point. But there's a problem, the horde's still roaming downstairs. The only way to the garage is through the old tech room on the west side." Jillian's face tensed with fear, but she nodded. "It won't be easy," he continued. "We move at nightfall, when it's darkest. If the horde hears us.. the garage door won't hold. So we have to be quiet, smart, and fast. You can do this. I know you can." Jillian met his eyes and nodded again, firmer this time.

"I'm ready."

As the sun began to set, casting long shadows across the ruined landscape, Derek and Jillian climbed back down from the roof. There was one way out. And no turning back. The slow, steady groans of the undead echoed faintly off the school walls. Derek and Jillian crept through the ruins of what had once been a bustling corridor, now reduced to rubble and rotting bodies. The horde had thinned. Most of them had wandered off in the hours since the battle, pulled away by noise, movement, or instinct. But a few, thirty, maybe more still prowled the ground floor like ghosts trapped in a memory.

Step by careful step, the pair moved through the halls. Jillian's hands trembled as she gripped a metal pipe scavenged from upstairs. Her face was pale, her body taut with fear and fatigue. Derek kept one eye on her and the other on the hallway ahead, leading her silently toward the tech room. It felt like it took hours. Every creak of a floorboard. Every accidental breath. But finally they made it. Derek pushed open the rusted door to the old tech room and slipped inside, guiding Jillian through. From there, a narrow corridor wound downward into the garage basement, a space once used for maintenance vehicles. It was quiet. Still. The overhead light flickered, revealing the old truck parked at the far end. "Still here," Derek said under his breath. He climbed in. The keys were still in the ignition. He turned them, and the engine purred to life. "Half a tank," he muttered. "It'll get us out."

Jillian stood nearby, arms folded tightly, avoiding his gaze. "Jillian," he said gently. She didn't reply. Still focused on the kiss on the roof. "You need to snap out of it. Look, it happened, all right? It was a kiss. Heat of the moment. No big deal. We've got bigger things to worry about."

She finally looked up, her cheeks red. "I know... I know. You're right. I'm sorry." She turned away quickly, climbing into the driver's seat of the truck. But in her heart... she wasn't sorry. Not at all.

Derek threw open the garage doors, startling a few roaming undead who had gathered. Two were thrown aside as the doors crashed outward. "Go, go, go!" Derek shouted as he dived into the truck. Jillian slammed the accelerator, and the vehicle roared forward crashing through the path, out the broken gates of the school, and west into the horizon.

They drove for hours Jillian keeping the wheel steady, Derek occasionally checking the map and watching for signs of danger. The sun dipped lower behind them. The road was mostly clear, but abandoned vehicles and wreckage forced detours through overgrown back roads and quiet streets. Then, the engine coughed. Spluttered. Stopped. Derek sighed. "That's it. We're dry." Jillian nodded, already climbing out.

They were maybe four miles from the new school, their fallback point. "We'll walk the rest," Derek said. For the next few hours, they trudged forward. Occasionally, they stopped at rusted-out cars, hoping for fuel or food. But luck wasn't on their side. One glove box yielded a pair of protein bars and some water bottles. It wasn't much but it was enough to keep them moving. The sun was near gone, casting pale gold light across the scattered clouds. That's when Jillian collapsed. "Whoa!" Derek caught her just before she hit the ground.

"I'm sorry," she whispered, exhausted. "I just... can't." Derek scanned the area. Nearby, behind a crumbled garden wall, stood a quiet house. In the overgrown yard, a small treehouse rested in the thick branches of a sturdy oak. Perfect. He lifted Jillian gently, carrying her across the grass. Up the ladder. Inside. The wooden shelter creaked slightly, but held. It was dusty, but dry. Derek laid her down on the thin sleeping mat someone had left behind maybe years ago, before the world fell apart.

"You sleep," he whispered. "We're close now. Just a little more."

She blinked slowly, half-asleep already. "Can I... can I cuddle you?"

Derek paused... then gave a small nod, arms open. "Yeah. Sure." She pressed into him, eyes closing, heartbeat finally slowing. And there they lay, exhausted, hungry, unsure of what came next—but alive. Together.

And close to home... or what was left of it.

Chapter 16 – The Search for a New Home

The morning air was cold and dry, still carrying the distant stench of smoke from the battle that destroyed their last haven. The survivors sat in silence as the bus rumbled down the broken tarmac road. Daryl's hands gripped the steering wheel tight, his eyes fixed on the road ahead. Behind him, Callum took charge, for now.

Jennifer sat beside Maggie near the rear of the bus, her eyes hollow and red-rimmed. She hadn't spoken much since Derek stayed behind. Callum understood. Jennifer was strong, but this had shaken her. Her husband is missing, her sister too, and half their friends dead. For now, leadership fell to him, and he bore the weight quietly.

The bus came to a slow halt outside the next school on their list, a large structure on the edge of a suburban district.

Daryl pulled the handbrake up and looked back. "We're here."

Callum, Maggie, and Old Bill stepped out first. The building looked promising with solid walls, no signs of movement. But as they approached, the truth hit them. The entire left side of the school was gone collapsed inward, likely from an old explosion or structural fire. From the road it had looked intact, but now…

"Bloody hell," Callum muttered.

Bill scratched his head and squinted. "I'm no expert," he said, smirking, "but I don't think that looks very safe." Maggie chuckled under her breath, but Callum wasn't amused.

"Back on the bus," he said. They regrouped quickly. Options were running thin. Tower block or prison.

The tower block offered height and vision, natural barriers, and potential to spot any threats before they got close. But if someone or something was already inside, clearing it would be a nightmare. Tight halls. Too many rooms. Too many unknowns.

The prison, though.. thick walls, one entrance, controlled gates. Razor wire still visible along the top fences. Built to keep people in, or out. Plus, Callum remembered they had a shot at restoring power. The security systems, cameras... it could be turned into a fortress.

Both had risks.

But they chose the prison.

As Callum prepared to signal the move, Jennifer stood suddenly, her voice cracking but clear. "We need to leave a note. For Derek and Jillian."

Callum nodded, already halfway through scribbling on a page torn from a notebook. "I was just doing that," he said, offering a small, reassuring smile. Jennifer gave a weak nod and sat back down, holding onto the hope that Derek and Jillian were still alive. Callum stepped out and wedged it on top of a rusted sign. It read: "School's not safe. Big hole inside. Went to prison. Will secure a section and wait for you." He folded it once so it wouldn't blow away, then returned to the bus. "Let's move."

They drove on, stopping only to siphon fuel from any abandoned vehicles they passed. They stuck to backroads, avoiding open highways and cities. The landscape was quiet now, no gunfire, no screams. Just the slow, haunting quiet of a world that had lost most of its people. As the prison finally came into view, its grey walls rising in the distance like a fortress of the old world, Callum stood near the front of the bus and said what everyone was thinking: "Let's hope to hell it's empty." And they rolled on, chasing a new home... and holding onto the hope that Derek would find them.

The bus groaned to a halt just outside the towering steel gates of the prison. A heavy silence blanketed the place, no wind, no birds, not even the distant shuffle of the undead. Just stillness. It was almost more unsettling than noise. Callum stood at the front, peering through the dust-caked windshield. "Too quiet," he muttered.

Jennifer shifted uneasily in her seat.

"Think the guards just left?" Maggie asked.

"Or worse," Bill replied with a grunt.

The guard house beside the gate looked untouched. No blood. No signs of a struggle. Just abandonment. Lee and Callum helped Daryl climb onto its roof, using a nearby pile of debris as a step. From there, Daryl jumped down behind the chained fence and kicked open the guard house door. Inside, the dust was thick but undisturbed. Cobwebs in the corners. A cracked mug is still on the desk. And on the far wall, behind a locked glass cabinet keys. A whole panel of them.

"Jackpot," Daryl whispered.

He raised the butt of his crossbow and smashed the glass, careful not to step on the shards. With a sweep of his hand, he grabbed the labeled key for the main gate and jogged outside. Manually unlocking the steel gate took effort. The rusted bolts groaned and resisted, but finally, the hinges shifted and the gate creaked open just wide enough for the bus to squeeze through. The vehicle rolled into the prison's outer car park, the sound of tires crunching over loose gravel echoing between the walls. Around them, a few abandoned cars sat buried in a layer of grime.

The inner walls loomed ahead, separating the parking lot from the actual prison compound. Its steel doors were locked shut but now they had keys. Daryl looked back at the rest. "We stay here tonight. Get some rest. Tomorrow, we check the inside."

No one argued.

Maggie and Bill wandered off to check the cars for supplies. A few unopened glove boxes yielded gloves, a bottle of painkillers, and an old chocolate bar, half-melted and stuck to the wrapper. No gold mines, but better than nothing.

Beside the guard house, a metal stairway led up to the perimeter wall. Daryl and Callum climbed it, rifles slung over their backs, and began a slow walk around the outer perimeter. The prison wasn't massive, but the security was solid. Razor wire still lined the top. No breaches. They unlocked each guard tower as they passed, sweeping them for supplies. A few had bottled water and dusty old rations, likely emergency kits from before the fall. By the time they returned, the sun was sinking fast.

"The wall's intact," Callum announced. "All towers locked but two. We'll use the ones above the guard house to keep watch."

Bill nodded. "I'll take the first shift with Daryl." As night settled over the prison, the group climbed back into the bus. It wasn't ideal, but it was still the safest shelter for now. Everyone piled in, exhausted and silent. Jennifer curled up in the back, clutching a worn photo of her and Derek.

Maggie sat cross-legged near the front, keeping her eyes on Callum. High above, Daryl and Bill took their positions in the towers. They'd found a pair of working walkie-talkies in a dusty locker, one of the few lucky finds. Bill tested it and gave a thumbs-up. The stars slowly blinked into the sky, cold and distant. The prison was quiet.

Bill leaned back in his chair and glanced over at Daryl. "Think we can secure this place?". Daryl was quiet for a moment, eyes scanning the dark tree line beyond the fence.

"It won't be easy," he said finally, "but if we can… we've got a real shot here. A fresh start. We just need to be smart."

Bill nodded, clutching the walkie. "Then we make it work." And with that, the prison, once a symbol of confinement, became their best chance at freedom.

Derek and Jillian awoke in the cramped warmth of the treehouse, the soft creaks of wood and the rustling breeze through the branches the only sounds. The sun was high overhead mid-afternoon, Derek guessed. They'd been out cold for over 12 hours. Groggy but alive, they devoured the last of the protein bars and sipped water from a salvaged bottle. Jillian looked better, still pale, but the rest and safety had clearly done her good.

"We're about an hour from the school," Derek said, brushing crumbs from his hands. "You good to go?"

Jillian nodded hesitantly. "I, uh… need to pee. But I can't… y'know… in front of you."

Derek chuckled softly and nodded, hopping down from the treehouse. "I'll check the house. Take your time."

Inside the house, Derek rummaged carefully through the drawers and closets. In a small jewelry box, he found a delicate crucifix necklace and a charm bracelet, probably once cherished by someone now long gone. He pocketed them, along with a few canned goods, a bottle of cough syrup, and a mostly intact lighter. It wasn't much, but every little bit helped. By the time he emerged, Jillian was climbing down the ladder, the bucket discreetly tucked away.

"All good?" he asked. She nodded, brushing her hair back. "Let's go."

The walk to the school was uneventful for the most part. A few straggling undead wandered the streets, but Derek dispatched them with swift, silent efficiency. They talked quietly as they moved, sharing memories, jokes, and the occasional moment of silence that spoke volumes. As the school came into view, their pace quickened.

"Maybe the bus is parked around the back," Jillian said.

"Yeah," Derek echoed. "Has to be."

But just a few blocks from the gates, Jillian stopped suddenly. "Derek... there's something I need to say."

He turned, concerned. "What's up?" "I'm worried about what happens when we see the others." She looked down. "About... the kiss."

Derek blinked. "The kiss?"

"I just... I feel guilty. What if someone finds out? What if—" "Jillian," he interrupted,

"No one will know. It was just us. And honestly? In that moment... anyone in your shoes might've done the same." She looked like she was about to respond when Derek leaned in and kissed her, gentle, quick, and certain. "There. Now it's both of us," he said with a soft smirk. "No guilt. Just a secret."

She laughed a real, unfiltered giggle. "Okay. It's our wee secret."

They reached the school, stepping through the shattered remnants of the front gate. The silence was eerie, but then Derek spotted the note pinned near the entrance. "School is not safe. Big hole inside. Have went to prison. Will secure a section and wait for you." Derek sighed. "The prison's over ten miles away. That's going to take time." Just then, a voice called from the side.

"Hello there."

A man in a priest's robe stepped from the shadows of the old church next door. He was middle-aged, with kind eyes and a cautious stance. "I'm Father Luke. I saw the group who left that note… I assume they're your people?"

Derek, one hand on his crossbow, nodded slowly. "Yeah. Where did you come from? Are you armed?"

"I have no weapons. The church is our home." The priest removed his robe, showing no weapons hidden beneath. "There are six others with me, two men, four women."

Derek narrowed his eyes. "Tell them to come out. Hands up." Father Luke didn't argue. He stepped back and called gently. One by one, the others emerged, hands raised. Jillian suddenly gasped.

"Vicki?!"

A woman near the back looked up, and her face lit up. "Jillian!" They ran into each other's arms, laughing and crying all at once. Then another man emerged, her husband, David. Jillian smiled warmly. "Hi, David. Derek, you remember Vicki."

"Yeah," Derek said, lowering his crossbow but still watchful.

Vicki was Jillian's life long friend, they grew up houses apart, went to the same nursery, primary and high school, they both had birthdays just 3 days apart. She had long blonde hair, and stunning blue eyes. They were inseparable growing up. Even after Vicki and David married, she was out with Jillian more than David.

Father Luke gestured toward the church. "Please. The streets aren't safe. Come inside." Inside, the church was humble and cold. Pews had been turned into makeshift beds. A few supplies, some blankets, candles, tins of food were all they had.

"They're barely surviving," Derek whispered to Jillian.

"We've been holding on," Father Luke admitted. "When I saw the bus, I thought about calling out... but there were too many. I didn't want to risk it." Derek looked around. Everyone looked tired, malnourished, and scared. These people weren't fighters. They were survivors by sheer will.

He went from person to person, talking briefly, learning their names and stories: David and Vicki: once happily married, now just trying to stay alive. Steven: a quiet man, early forties, with a limp and a haunted look. Ashley, Sarah, and Mary: young women from the local area, all no older than thirty, holding each other close for comfort and protection.

Derek stood back, arms crossed, as Jillian spoke softly to her old friend. This wasn't part of the plan but then, nothing in this world was anymore. Still, as Derek looked around, he knew what came next. They were going to the prison and now they weren't going alone.

Chapter 17 – Ashes of Blantyre

The morning after the battle, Kinross was unusually still. The air carried a smoky tang, remnants of the chaos that had erupted the day before. In the heart of the fortified compound, deep within the municipal building turned war room, Ellis sat in his office. The sharp crackle of a fire in the hearth was the only sound, until the heavy door creaked open. Bellamy stepped in, his ever-loyal second-in-command Munroe trailing behind.

Ellis looked up, his expression unreadable. "I want the school checked," he said without preamble. "Any survivors... bring them to me."

Bellamy nodded once. "Consider it done."

Outside the compound, two trucks were readied. Bellamy assembled a small strike force of trusted men. The plan was simple but calculated. "Team One," Bellamy explained, pointing to a map, "you draw away any of the dead still lingering. Blast the horn, make noise, lead them away down the east end of Blantyre. Team Two, that's us,we'll hang back and observe for movement. Anyone recently turned could still be shambling nearby. We don't go in until it's clear."

The drive to the school was eerily quiet, the streets deserted except for the occasional lone figure, undead and aimless. When they reached the edge of the school grounds, the damage was clear. Smoke still curled from the broken windows. The eastern side of the building was blackened and collapsed in places, fire having done its brutal work.

Team One pulled ahead, laying on the truck horn. The few remaining undead stirred and began to follow the noise, stumbling after the moving vehicle. Five minutes later, Team Two arrived. Bellamy and Munroe stepped out, leaving Raven behind in the driver's seat, engine humming and ready for a quick getaway.

"Keep it running," Bellamy told her. Raven nodded silently, her dark hair tied back, eyes sharp and unblinking on the mirrors. She looked young, but there was steel in the way she gripped the wheel.

Bellamy and Munroe entered the building carefully, rifles raised. The smell hit them immediately, char, rot, and death. They passed twisted metal, scorched furniture, and blackened corpses. Among the dead were both zombies and humans, many too far gone to identify. They moved deeper into the ruins, clearing room by room. Bellamy stepped over what was once a makeshift barricade, now reduced to ash and rubble.

"No sign of Derek," Munroe said quietly.

Bellamy grunted, kneeling beside a recently turned corpse. It still wore a necklace, now fused to its burned skin. "They fought here. Hard." It wasn't until they reached the rear of the school that Munroe noticed it, garage doors wide open, scorched but intact. He crouched low and examined the ground.

"Fresh tire marks," he said. "Someone drove out of here. Fast."

Bellamy joined him and nodded after a moment. "Don't mention that in the report. Not yet."

Munroe gave him a sideways glance. "Why?"

"Because," Bellamy said, standing again, "Ellis wants closure. If he thinks Derek might still be out there, he'll waste more men chasing a ghost." Munroe didn't respond, just followed Bellamy back to the waiting vehicle. They got in and Raven drove back to new Kinross.

Munroe was Bellamy's second in command, a short man, in his late thirties, loyal to the core. He had known Bellamy since their army days, he enlisted when he was 18 and Bellamy took him under his wing. He was the calming voice when Bellamy lost it.

Back at Kinross, they went straight into Ellis's office. He stood when they entered, impatience thick in the air. "Well?" he asked.

Bellamy didn't flinch. "The school is gone. Fire gutted most of it. There were bodies everywhere, some recently turned. No sign of Derek or any living person."

Ellis's eyes narrowed. "Are you certain?"

Bellamy nodded. "Given the size of the horde and the damage... surviving that would've been a miracle."

"What do you think Munroe?" Ellis said.

Munroe looked Ellis square in the face, Bellamy worried what he would say. "If they survived that they best put the lottery on." Replied Munroe.

Ellis sat slowly, a thin smile curling on his lips. "Then our problem has solved itself." Munroe looked at Bellamy but said nothing. Outside, the smoke still rose in the distance,silent witness to a battle lost, and to survivors who may not be as dead as Ellis believed.

Back at the church, the tension had eased just slightly. Derek had finished explaining where he and Jillian were headed, the prison, where the others had gone. He extended the invitation to Father Luke and his small group, giving them a choice. All of them agreed to come along without hesitation, except Stephen. He stood still, eyes low, gripping the handle of an old hunting knife.

"I appreciate the offer," he said quietly, "but I can't leave. My son and daughter... they're still out there. We were at another camp, I was away foraging when we heard the screams, by the time we got back no one was left, we put down the zombies but none were my kids."

Derek nodded solemnly. "You're sure they made it?"

Stephen looked up, his expression one of painful determination. "I don't know. But I need to be sure."

Father Luke stepped forward. "Stephen... your children are likely with God now. Holding onto false hope only delays your own peace."

Stephen turned, eyes hard. "With respect, Father, peace doesn't matter until I know the truth." The silence that followed said everything.

Derek gave him a steady look. "I understand. I really do."

A voice cut through the stillness, Mary, timid but hopeful. "I have a car. My house is only four blocks from here. It still works—seven seats. We could fit everyone... with a squeeze."

Derek's eyes lit up with cautious optimism. "That could save us a hell of a walk. Keys?"

"In my house," she said. "But... my husband's there. He... turned. I saw him before I left."

Derek nodded gently. "Then we'll deal with him. Respectfully."

"I'm coming too," David said, standing tall. Derek studied him for a moment, then finally gave a small nod.

"Fine. But you follow orders. No hero moves."

David nodded, gripping a rusted crowbar he'd fashioned into a weapon. The plan was simple: scavenge house to house for supplies on the way to Mary's place. The streets weren't entirely empty, but the few undead they saw were dispatched quickly. Jillian and Derek moved like clockwork. Even David managed to take down a straggler, pride flashing briefly on his face. They reached Mary's house. The door creaked open to silence. No groans. No movement. "Clear" Derek said, voice low. They moved through the home room by room, living room, kitchen, upstairs bedrooms.

No sign of Mary's husband. "Maybe he wandered off," Jillian suggested, half-hopeful. They found the keys on a hook by the front door. As they stepped outside—David screamed. A zombie lunged from behind the side of the porch, grabbing his arm and snapping its teeth inches from his throat. Derek didn't hesitate, he rammed the creature into the pavement and crushed its skull against the curb with a sickening crack. Jillian looked down, wincing. The clothes were familiar. Mary's husband.

"We tell her he was laid to rest, respectfully," Derek said softly. "Knife to the back of the head. Peaceful." David just nodded, shaken.

They loaded the car, a weathered estate wagon with enough seats, barely. The engine started on the second turn. A small miracle in itself. Back at the church, the rest were ready. They piled in tightly, bags on laps, elbows pressed to ribs. But it would do. Before they left, Derek turned to Stephen and handed him a small pistol fitted with a makeshift silencer. "Three rounds left. Make 'em count."

Stephen took it with trembling hands. "You didn't have to"

"I'll come back," Derek said. "One month. If you've found your kids, I'll take you all. If not, your space is still waiting." They shook hands, a moment of respect between men forged by loss and fire.

The car pulled away slowly, then picked up speed down the road. Jillian leaned out the window. "Prison, here we come!" she called, trying to sound cheerful.

Derek smirked. "Never thought I'd be happy to hear that." Stephen stood outside the church, a lone figure waving as the car disappeared over the hill and into the unknown.

After a few hours of driving the prison loomed ahead like a sleeping beast of concrete and steel. Its towers cast long shadows over the empty road as Derek slowed the car. They'd made it, tired, cramped, and sore but they were alive. Jillian shifted in her seat, her eyes wide with nerves.

"So... this is home now?" Derek didn't answer right away. He stared through the windshield, scanning for signs of life.

"It'll do."

Chapter 18 – New Walls, New Rules

The morning haze was just beginning to lift over the prison yard. A chilling wind whistled through the chain-link fencing, carrying with it the scent of damp earth and rusted metal.

Daryl stood in the guard tower, binoculars in hand, scanning the tree line. Down below, in the rec room-turned-planning space, Callum, Jennifer, and Maggie were bent over the prison map. A-block remained sealed, but they needed a real plan to clear it safely.

"If we can lure them out one by one through the corridor…" Maggie began.

Jennifer shook her head. "Too risky. The numbers are too high. What if we block off the far end and funnel them toward the courtyard?"

"Could work," Callum replied. "We'd need noise, though. Something to get their attention without drawing in every deadhead for miles."

Before Maggie could respond, the door to the block slammed open. Liam burst in, breathless, eyes wide. "Derek's at the gate!" Everyone froze. Jennifer's heart skipped.

Callum stood straight. "What?"

"I saw the car. It's him. Jillian's with him. He's here!"

Callum bolted for the stairwell without a word, Maggie and Jennifer right behind him. At the gate.

The car rolled to a stop at the outer gate. The same one Daryl had forced open just days earlier. Derek stepped out slowly, motioning for the others to stay put. "Cover me," he said to Jillian as he moved toward the gatehouse, but before he even reached it a voice rang out from above.

"That's close enough, cowboy." Derek looked up, Daryl stood on one of the watchtowers, crossbow aimed but not tense.

"Daryl!" he shouted, as he approached the gate.

"Holy shit," Daryl muttered, lowering the weapon. "Get Jennifer and Callum down here, now!" he barked into a walkie-talkie. Moments later, the outer gate creaked open. Callum stood there, arms crossed but his face lit up with disbelief. "You made it..."

Derek stepped forward, exhausted but grinning. "Told you I'd catch up." The two men clasped hands, a firm grip filled with shared survival and unspoken brotherhood. Jillian smiled as Jennifer appeared behind Callum. Her eyes welled with tears.

"Jen..." Jillian ran to her and hugged her tight, both women crying softly.

"You're safe," Jennifer whispered.

Callum's eyes swept the rest of the group as they got out of the car. "Friends of yours?"

"Yeah," Derek replied. "Some good people. Father Luke, David, Vicki, Mary, Ashley, and Sarah. They need food, rest, and safety."

"You'll get all three," Callum nodded. "We're securing the place one wing at a time."

"Where's Bill and Maggie?" Derek asked.

"Inside," Callum replied. "Scouting the east wing."

Inside the prison walls, the group was shown to a cleared cell block, C-Block. Cleaned out, barred windows open for air, cots set up in the cells. It was rough, but it was a sanctuary compared to the chaos outside. Father Luke looked around solemnly.

"Never thought I'd find comfort in a place like this."

"None of us did," said Daryl, handing him a bottle of water. "But it's walls and doors that lock. That's more than most can say."

Later that evening, as the group ate scavenged rations by firelight in the prison yard, Derek sat with Callum and Daryl on overturned crates, watching the sun set behind the towers.

"This place," Callum said, "we can make it work."

"We have to," Derek added. "Too many people counting on it now."

"Any sign of Ellis?" Daryl asked.

Derek shook his head. "Not yet. But he won't give up."

"We'll be ready," Callum said. "Let him come."

Behind them, laughter echoed from the yard as Jillian and Jennifer sat with the others. Vicki was showing Ashley how to start a fire with flint. For a moment, there was peace. Derek leaned back and looked at the rising moon above the prison walls. The apocalypse hadn't ended but for the first time in a long while, it felt like they had a fighting chance.

Chapter 18 continued: securing the prison(flashback)

The morning after Callum's group arrived they head into the prison to secure it, armed with the keys they found in the security gatehouse they can lock and unlock any door they wish.They stepped cautiously into the main lobby, the air heavy with dust and silence. Sunlight filtered through the high, grime-streaked windows, casting long shadows across the tiled floor. The map behind the reception desk was faded but still legible, showing the four wings clearly, A-block, B-block, C-block, and the east wing that housed the administrative areas and essential services.

"This place could actually work," Callum muttered, eyeing the thick walls and reinforced doors. "If we can secure each section, we could have real shelter here."

"No more sleeping in the damn bus," Bill grunted in agreement.

They split into pairs, sticking to the plan. C-block was first, closest, and reportedly only had four inmates when the world ended. Callum and Daryl led the way while Maggie and Bill stayed alert by the entrance. Torches flickered as they approached the barred entrance. Daryl rattled the gate, the metallic clatter echoing down the corridor. For a few tense moments, nothing happened. Then, one undead figure appeared, dragging its foot as it emerged from a cell.

Daryl took it out quickly with his crossbow, the bolt lodging deep into the zombie's skull.

"Clear the cells," Callum ordered.

They moved through cautiously, one door at a time. No more zombies. Just quiet and dust.

"All clear," Callum shouted back. "Bring them in!"

Maggie waved the others forward, and soon enough, the rest of the group were settling into the empty cells. Jennifer claimed one near the front, Maggie and Bill took two opposite each other. Anne and Callum quietly slid into one together, finally able to share a moment of peace. Daryl gave them a knowing look but didn't say a word. He stayed alert, the de facto leader now that Derek was gone.

With C-block secured, the next objective was B-block. Maggie and Bill joined Daryl while Jennifer tagged along, wanting to help. According to the paperwork, B-block had been overcrowded, a red flag in a place like this. Same strategy. Daryl rattled the bars, then stepped back. It took only seconds. Seven undead shuffled into view, groaning behind the gates. "Ready?" he asked. The team nodded. Gates opened. Bolts flew. Knives swung. When the last one dropped, they fanned out into the block and cleared it cell by cell. It was tiring work, but they finished it with no injuries. Another block safe.

Then came A-block.

Even before they reached the entrance, the stench hit them. Foul, thick, and clinging to the air. "Out of use due to incident." "Maybe we should block this entrance and come back later?" Jennifer says.

"No arguments here," Maggie said, already dragging a metal filing cabinet in front of the gate. "Let's make sure these bastards stay in." With A-block sealed and reinforced, they turned their attention to the final wing, the admin area. It was different. More open, more offices than cells. The kitchen and rec rooms had been untouched since the outbreak. They moved quietly, dispatching a few lone zombies along the way..

Finally, after nearly 6 hours, they reached the last room, the kitchen. Callum placed a hand on the swinging door then froze as a voice rang out from

"Open that door and I'll shoot!" Everyone froze.

Callum raised his voice calmly. "We're not here to hurt you. Just clearing the building."

"I've got one bullet left," the voice trembled. 'Don't make me use it."

Daryl replied . "We're not a threat. We've got food, water. You're welcome to join us."

A long pause. Then, slowly, the door creaked open. A thin man in his fifties stepped out, holding a revolver with shaking hands. Greasy apron, hollow cheeks, but alert eyes.

"I'm Reggie," he said. "Used to be the cook here. Been locked in the pantry since this all started."

Jennifer stepped up. "Well, Reggie, how do you feel about cooking for a group again?"

The revolver lowered slightly. "If you've got ingredients, I've got recipes," said Reggie.

The group chuckled, the tension breaking at last. As they made their way back to C-block,Reggie in tow the prison felt less like a ruin and more like the beginnings of a real home. A place to regroup, recover, and maybe.. rebuild.

Reggie sat on an upturned crate in c block, a half-empty tin of beans in one hand and a distant look in his eyes. "Wasn't always like this," he muttered, shaking his head. "The guards... they were scared, same as everyone else. Orders came down, said to put every inmate into one block. Didn't matter who they were, murderers, thieves, low-level junkies, they all got shoved into A-block."

He looked up at the group as they listened in silence. "They locked 'em in... and then they left. Just walked out the front gate. Took what they could carry and never looked back. Only two of 'em stayed, McIntyre and Hodge. Said it was their duty to protect what was left." Reggie sighed. "They lasted maybe a week before the inmates turned on them. After that, it was just screaming. Then silence."

No one spoke for a moment. The weight of what had happened there, what the place had endured, hung heavy in the air.

Callum broke the silence. "They locked them in to die..."

Reggie nodded slowly. "Yeah. Like animals."

That night, the group secured C-block tight. The steel doors were shut and locked. Daryl and Maggie took turns on watch at the entrance while Callum and Anne finally got some real rest, curled up in the corner of their cell. Bill sat quietly sharpening a blade, wishing he was back in his wee shop. He used to run a small store that sold hunting gear, crossbows, bow's, knives. He ran that shop for twenty years. Reggie, surprisingly, snored in one of the guard bunks, exhaustion overtaking him after weeks in hiding.

Chapter 19 – A-Block (Back to present day)

The sun rose behind the grey clouds, casting a dull hue over the prison yard. Dew clung to the rusted bars and makeshift barricades as the group gathered, ready for the toughest task yet, clearing A-block.

Callum ran over the plan one last time with Derek as they examined the rough sketch drawn on a board inside the admin wing. "There's thirty-five, maybe forty in there. All packed in. The idea is to open the door to the yard, get them to funnel out single-file through the path we've made. That should give us a better shot at thinning them out."

Derek nodded, arms folded. "Makes sense. Keep the spread tight, keep control."

Callum pointed at the map. "You and Daryl take roof positions. Good angles, clear shots. Lee's up in the tower, he's solid. Maggie and Bill are on the ground, just off to each side of the fence. If any get through, they've got backup. Jennifer and Anne will handle unlocking the yard gate, but—"

David stepped forward. "Let me do it." All eyes turned to him.

"I used to run track. I think I'll be faster than Jennifer and Anne. If this goes sideways, I've got the best chance of getting out alive."

Vicki frowned. "David, no. You're not trained for this."

"I know," he said softly. "But I can help. I want to help."

Derek glanced around. No one else objected. "Alright. It's your call. But when you open that door, don't stop. Straight to the tower, no heroics."

The group moved into position. Hours of planning, barricade building, and scrounging supplies had led to this moment. Metal fences formed a crude funnel from the A-block door to the yard, reinforced with poles, desks, even tied bedsheets. It would hold at least for a while.

From the roof, Derek and Daryl lay prone, rifles ready. Lee adjusted the scope on his rifle from the tower, calm and focused. Maggie and Bill knelt behind the fence, eyes sharp, nerves taut. Jennifer gave David a quick hug, her face pale but composed. Anne offered a thumbs-up, trying to hide her fear. Derek's voice crackled through the radio.

"Positions, everyone. David, it's on you. Open that door and run like hell." David gave a nod, exhaled, and sprinted to the A-block door.

The sound of the lock turning echoed like thunder. As the door creaked open, the stench hit him first, rot, sweat, death. Then came the growls. Moans. Shuffling. He didn't wait. He turned and ran. Behind him, the first of the undead lurched through the doorway, blinking in the grey light. Then more. Dozens. Crashing and stumbling into the funnel. Gunfire cracked across the yard. One, two, five, ten, undead dropped in heaps as they pressed into the trap. The narrow corridor forced them forward in clumps, easy pickings for the sharpshooters above. Maggie and Bill fired in short bursts, conserving ammo.

David reached the tower, breath ragged, and scrambled up the ladder. Jennifer grabbed his arm and pulled him the last few feet. "You did it!" she shouted. But it wasn't over. The zombies kept coming.

The makeshift tunnel creaked under the pressure. A desk leg snapped, sending a section sagging.

"Left side's dipping!" Callum yelled over the radio. Derek zeroed in on the densest part of the horde and unloaded. "Dropping the ones on the left side!" One by one they fell and the pressure eased. The fence held. One by one, the zombies fell until silence took over. No growls. No moans. Just the heavy breaths of the living and the echo of spent shells hitting concrete.

Derek stood slowly, wiping his brow. "That's it."

Callum raised his radio. "All clear. A-block is clear."

A cheer erupted, tired but triumphant. They had done it. But as the smoke cleared, Derek looked down at the pile of bodies and knew this was just one battle. The war wasn't over. Not by a long shot.

The bodies from A-block were piled high in the yard, doused with fuel, and set ablaze. The acrid smoke of burning corpses curled into the dull afternoon sky, a thick black signal of the grim work completed. The group stood back, some covering their noses, others simply staring in silence. The stench was horrific, the scent of death baked into the concrete walls. A-block would need a serious clean but that could wait. Right now, their focus was survival.

Inside the rec room, the group gathered around a large plastic table. A sense of relief hung in the air, tempered, but real. The prison was secure. For the first time since the world ended, they had walls that wouldn't collapse, gates that locked, and a place to call their own. But safety was only the beginning.

"We need to think ahead," Derek said, his voice cutting through the low murmurs. "Food, water, medicine, ammo. If we don't plan now, we'll end up like every other group we've met, desperate or dead."

Daryl nodded. "Med bay's basically stripped. Maybe enough for a cut and a cold, but nothing major."

Reggie, leaning against the far wall, perked up with a small grin. "I don't think we'll have much of a problem with food or weapons, actually." That got everyone's attention. He motioned for them to follow him and led them down a stairwell behind a locked utility door, this one's not marked on any of the maps they'd found. The air grew cooler as they descended into the dimly lit basement. Dust coated every surface, but Reggie moved with confidence. "This part of the prison was only known to staff and guards. It doesn't show on any blueprint or map." Reggie explains. He pushed open a heavy steel door. Inside was every survivalist's fantasy.

An armoury.

Rows of rifles, shotguns, pistols, crates of ammunition stacked like bricks. Vests, batons, riot shields. It was enough to outfit a small militia.

Bill let out a low whistle. "Jesus... this is a bloody goldmine."

Jennifer's eyes were wide. "Where the hell did all this come from?" "

Back when the world still worked," Reggie said, "they were expecting riots or even full-on takeovers. This was the backup plan. Guess it's ours now."

Derek grinned. "Well damn, Reggie. I could kiss you right now."

Reggie took a step back, raising both hands. "Whoa now, I'm flattered, but I don't swing that way, Derek."

The room broke out in laughter, the tension easing for a moment. Even Derek chuckled, shaking his head. But Reggie wasn't done. "One more thing." He led them through another door at the far end of the armoury, the lock rusted but intact. Inside was a massive walk-in fridge freezer, humming with preserved life. Canned goods, vacuum-sealed meats, bottled water, vegetables in crates, dry rations stacked to the ceiling. It was cold, clean, and pristine. "There's enough here, to last a few years. As long as we ration and don't waste it." said Reggie.

Derek stared in disbelief. "You're serious?"

Reggie just shrugged. "Dead serious."

Derek turned, and slapped Reggie's shoulder. "You've just made my bloody week."

"Still not letting you kiss me, mate." Reggie says as another round of laughter rolled through the group.

Back upstairs, with hope now a tangible thing, Derek handed two sets of keys to Maggie and Jennifer. "You two are in charge of this. Both rooms. Do inventory, keep it logged. If something goes missing, I want to know."

Jennifer looked at Maggie and nodded. "We're on it."

"I've got the second key," Derek said. "No one else gets in without one of us."

The group slowly disbanded, drifting to their new rooms, makeshift bunks, and personal corners of this new home. For the first time in months, there was warmth in the air that had nothing to do with fire. They had walls. Weapons. Food. And now, finally, a future. All they had to do... was make it feel like home.

Later that evening, the fire outside had died down to smouldering ash, but inside the prison walls, things were just beginning to stir again. In the rec room, maps were laid out on the table with a plan coming together.

Reggie leaned over and tapped his finger on a small dot just off the main road. "There's a village about five miles out, Crossford. A small place, maybe sixty people lived there back in the day. Not much to look at, but it had a pharmacy and a medical centre. Not state of the art, but shelves packed with meds and supplies."

That got everyone's attention.

"If it's not looted," Daryl said, "we could find bandages, antibiotics, maybe even painkillers or morphine."

"It's worth the risk," Derek agreed. "We need a proper medical stash in case anyone gets hurt. That med bay upstairs is a joke." The plan came together quickly. Daryl would lead the run, taking Callum, Lee, and Maggie. As they gathered their gear, Jennifer stepped forward, ready to volunteer.

"I'll come too," she said, slinging her crossbow over her shoulder.

But Derek raised a hand. "No. I want you here."

Jennifer frowned, "Why?"

"Because I trust you to keep things running while I'm not here. Keep Reggie out of trouble, make sure no one gets the stupid idea to sneak off," he said with a small smirk. "Besides, we need you here in case anyone comes knocking." Jennifer gave him a reluctant nod.

Two more stepped forward, Ashley and Sarah. "We'll go," Sarah said. "Yeah, we've not been on a run yet," Ashley added. Derek looked them over, then nodded slowly.

Ashley and Sarah lived in the village where they met Derek, both in their mid twenties. Ashley had short ginger hair, Sarah was taller by a few inches, long golden blonde hair. They were neighbors alongside Mary. The 3 of them went to church every Sunday. Done the gardens and helped out in their small community.

As they loaded up the car, Derek pulled Callum aside quietly. "Keep an eye on them. Sarah and Ashley… they're not the best shots. Not much use in a brawl either. I don't want anyone slowing you down, but I sure as hell don't want them getting killed."

"I'll watch them," Callum promised.

"Good," Derek clapped him on the back. "Be smart."

With that, Liam opened the main gate and watched the vehicle vanish down the road toward Crossford, then sealed it shut behind them, rifle in hand as he returned to watch duty in the tower. The rest of the survivors were spread out, some in the yard, others tidying up the mess inside A-block, scrubbing the blood from walls and scraping remains off the floor.

Back inside, the prison was quieter than it had been all day. In C-block, Derek and Jennifer walked together in silence. They passed the occupied cells, then climbed the stairs to the far end of the upper tier, a row of cells no one had claimed yet. He opened the door to one. It was empty, but clean. Quiet. Isolated.

He turned to Jennifer, pulled her close, and kissed her. Deeply. It was the first real moment they'd had since the world turned upside down. Their hands roamed with urgency, tearing at clothes like the world might end again at any second. They fell into the bunk, tangled in each other, making love for the first time in what felt like forever. For a brief, blissful moment, nothing else existed but the two of them.

But in the cell next to theirs, Jillian sat on the bunk, back against the wall, hands curled tightly into her lap. She didn't move. She didn't make a sound. But she heard it all. Her heart pounded in her chest, not from fear but from something far more complicated. Jealousy twisted in her gut. She hated it, but she couldn't stop it. She wanted Derek. She didn't know when it started, or why. Maybe it was because he was strong, maybe because he gave her hope when everything else was dark. Or maybe because he was the one person she felt safe with.

But he was married. To her sister. She knew it was wrong. But knowing didn't make the feelings go away. She pressed her head against the cold wall and closed her eyes. Trying not to cry. Trying not to feel. Trying not to listen.

The car rumbled down the cracked country road, tires crunching over stray gravel and wind sweeping across the open fields. After nearly an hour of driving, the small village of Crossford came into view, bathed in golden morning sunlight. It was quiet. Too quiet. They passed boarded-up houses, empty streets, and a rusted swing creaking in the breeze. No movement. No sound.

"Place seems empty," Maggie said, squinting out the window, her hand resting on her pistol.

"Everyone knows the drill," Callum replied, glancing into the wing mirrors. "Be ready for anything."

They pulled into the cracked, weed-strewn medical centre car park. Grass poked through the concrete, and faded signs still flapped in the wind.

Daryl stepped out and stretched his back. "Alright, we stick together. Pharmacy first, then the main centre. Let's make it quick."

The group moved cautiously down the short path to the pharmacy next door. Its windows were dusty but intact. Daryl pushed open the front door with a soft creak. Inside, the place was eerily intact, papers still sat on the counter, posters hung on the walls, and a lone zombie in a white lab coat stood behind the desk, swaying gently. As if waiting to serve the next customer. Daryl didn't hesitate, one silenced shot, and it dropped.

"Jackpot," Maggie breathed, stepping forward. The shelves were still stocked, painkillers, antibiotics, bandages, even asthma inhalers. Everyone grabbed what they could, stuffing supplies into their backpacks. For twenty straight minutes they worked, scouring every aisle, but by the end of it, the important medicines were mostly gone. The group had done well, but the critical supplies, antivirals, insulin, stronger antibiotics, were scarce.

"Alright," Daryl said, "onto the medical centre."

They crossed the street and approached the larger building. Its revolving glass door was dusty but still surprisingly functional. With a gentle push, it creaked into motion.

Inside, the centre smelled of disinfectant and decay. Lights flickered overhead as they moved room by room, exam rooms, storage closets, offices, grabbing anything useful. Then they came to a door marked PRIVATE. It was locked. "Hello?" Callum knocked once, then waited. No response.

Daryl stepped up. "Stand back." With a solid boot to the centre of the door, it cracked and swung inward. The stench hit them first, rotting flesh.

Inside the room was a makeshift barricade, and behind it, a single zombie nurse crouched in the corner, gnawing at a long-dead arm. Daryl took her out quickly, eyes scanning the room. This had once been a treatment bay, but now it was more like a last refuge. A mattress was pushed against the wall, empty pill bottles littered the floor, and a notebook lay open on the desk beside a half-empty bottle of water.

Callum picked it up. "She tried to hold out here... last entry says she locked herself in after the others turned. She must have starved to death."

They all stood in silence for a moment. Maggie exhaled. "Let's finish up and get the hell out of here."

They moved quickly, grabbing what was left, some gauze, a box of surgical masks, a few sealed IV bags. Then, with their packs heavy and the village still eerily silent, they made their way back to the car.

As they drove off, the wind picked up, rustling the long grass behind them. No one noticed the curtain in one of the nearby houses shift slightly. They weren't alone. As the team left Crossford, the sun still high in the sky, a red flare suddenly shot up into the air from behind them.

Maggie slammed on the brakes. "Did anyone else see that?"

"It came from back in Crossford," Callum said, squinting out the rear window. "That was a signal. Or a warning." Sarah looked uneasy.

"Maybe it was just an old flare.. maybe it's nothing." Ashley added quickly, "We should go home. We've got what we came for."

But Daryl shook his head. "Flares don't fire themselves, someone either wants us to know they are there or it was a signal."

"I agree," Callum said. "Someone's out there. Might be in trouble."

Maggie nodded and looked at the others. "Three votes to two. Sorry, ladies."

She spun the car around and headed back, tires skidding lightly on the tarmac as they made a quick U-turn. They parked a few houses away from the medical centre, careful not to draw too much attention, and locked the vehicle behind them. Weapons ready, they moved in pairs, eyes sharp, checking each house near the centre. The streets were still empty, too quiet, no movement, no sounds of the dead. Just birds and the distant whistle of wind through broken windows.

After nearly fifteen minutes of searching, they had found nothing. Disappointed and uneasy, the group began heading back toward the car when Ashley froze in place. "There!" she gasped, pointing up at a second-story window of a nearby house. A shadow had moved, a figure ducking out of sight just as she pointed. The team dropped low, instantly alert.

"You sure?" Callum whispered. Ashley nodded.

"Positive." Daryl raised his weapon. "Let's check it out. Carefully."

The house was a two-story detached, worn and quiet. The curtains in the upper window shifted, just barely, catching Ashley's attention. Daryl took point with Maggie and Callum close behind. Ashley and Sarah stayed toward the rear, nerves showing but staying silent. They approached the front door cautiously. Daryl pushed it, unlocked. It creaked open slowly, revealing a dusty hallway with scattered toys and faded family photos on the wall. It was a home, not just a house, once full of life. Room by room, they cleared the ground floor. Nothing. Daryl signaled toward the staircase. Step by step, they climbed. At the top, three doors. One slightly ajar.

Daryl took the lead and opened the door quickly, weapon raised.Inside, a man stood in the corner with his hands up.

"Don't shoot," he said quickly. "I'm not infected." The man looked to be in his late forties, thin, unshaven, eyes hollow but sharp. He stood in what used to be a child's bedroom, stickers on the walls, small drawings pinned to a corkboard.

Maggie lowered her weapon a bit, watching him carefully. "You fire the flare?"

He nodded. "I saw your car.. figured you were survivors. Thought maybe you'd help."

Callum stepped in beside her, keeping his bow ready. "Why the flare? Trying to draw attention?"

"No. Just trying to reach people. I was with a group for a while. We found a church a few towns south. Stayed there for some time. But I left.. I came back here. This was my home. I was hoping to find my kids." Ashley and Sarah entered the room behind them. Ashley froze the moment she saw the man. Her eyes widened.

"Stephen?" she said, her voice barely above a whisper. The man turned sharply, eyes locking on her. He looked stunned.

"Ashley..?" Sarah gasped and stepped closer, recognition dawning. Stephen stepped forward slowly, voice shaky. "You two.. I thought I'd never see you again."

Ashley smiled, eyes misty. "Did you find your kids?"

Stephen shook his head. "Unfortunatly no. I had hoped they might have tried to make it home but no one has been here for months."

Callum looked between them, confused. "You know him?"

"Yeah," Sarah said quietly. "We were all together at the church before we parted ways."

Stephen nodded. "We all went different directions. I'm just glad to have found you again."

Daryl relaxed slightly but kept his tone firm. "You sick? Bitten?"

Stephen shook his head. "No. Just tired. Hungry. I've been on my own for days."

Maggie exhaled. "We have a place. Secure enough for now. If you come with us, you follow the rules. No second chances."

Stephen nodded solemnly. "Understood."

As they led him downstairs and out to the car, Ashley glanced back at the house, the place Stephen had once called home. Empty now, like so many others. Before they left, Stephen put a note on the fridge, telling his kids to wait here in the secret hiding place, he would come back.

Back in the car, Sarah sat beside Stephen, a smile tugging at the corner of her mouth. It was good to find someone from the recent past, even if the world had changed.

Maggie put the car into gear. "Let's get back before dark."

As they drove off, Stephen stared out the window, silently hoping that wherever they were going, it might offer more than just shelter. It might offer hope.

Chapter 20 – The Future

With Daryl, Callum, Maggie, Ashley, and Sarah away, the rest of the group turned their attention to making the prison feel less like a fortress and more like a home. Jennifer and Jillian approached Derek, their faces serious.

"Morale's low," Jennifer said quietly. "We're all living in a prison, after all."

Derek nodded, understanding the weight of her words. "I'm open to any ideas use have?"

Just then, Liam stepped in. "We could freshen the place up. There's a hardware store not far from here. We could check it out, get paint, pictures, anything to make it feel less like a prison and more like home. We could even get gardening tools. Make a garden out in the dirt yard."

Derek thought for a moment, then agreed. "Sounds good. I'll set up a team." He looked around the room. "Bill, Ross, Liam, and myself will go."

Jillian raised her hand with a smirk. "Can I come too? Guys don't have much of a knack for paint colors or accessories."

Jennifer smiled. "Okay. We'll need the extra hands. Plus, it's a stronger group leaving, safer that way."

Earlier, they'd managed to get one of the old cars in the prison's car park started after securing the building. Now, the team began loading supplies into it. Before they left, Derek pulled Jennifer aside.

He kissed her softly and said, "You're in charge until I'm back." Jillian looked away, her face a mixture of frustration and something deeper, but she stayed silent.

The drive was quiet at first, the mood light, almost hopeful. But as they turned a corner past an old shopping strip, Ross suddenly slowed the car and pulled to a stop outside a colourful, faded storefront. Derek frowned. "Why are we stopping?"

Ross pointed to the sign above: Kidz Planet – Toys, Games & More! "All the kids have back at the prison is one worn-out ball," Ross said. "Maybe we pick up a few things. Give them something to smile about."

Derek hesitated, then nodded. "Alright. Quick stop."

The store wasn't large. Bill and Liam stayed outside on lookout while Derek, Ross, and Jillian slipped inside with empty bags. Dust coated most of the shelves, but the place had been untouched. Shelves still stocked with dolls, action figures, puzzles, and games. They moved quickly, filling a trolley with as much as they could carry, board games, teddy bears, toy cars. As they turned to leave, a loud clatter echoed from the back of the store. A toy had fallen. Weapons instantly raised, the three spun toward the sound.

"Come out or we shoot!" Derek barked.

Two small figures emerged from behind a display, one after the other. A girl, maybe ten or eleven, her hands raised high. Behind her, a younger boy clutched her arm, clearly terrified.

"Don't shoot!" the girl pleaded. "We're just kids!" "My name's Lexi," she said, voice trembling. "This is Jack. My brother."

Jillian lowered her weapon slowly. "Where are your parents?" she asked, firm but gentle.

Lexi shook her head. "We got separated from our dad a few months ago. This... this was our favourite store. We came here hoping he'd come back for us. We've been living off sweets and juice since."

Ross glanced at Derek. He nodded silently.

"We're taking you with us," Derek said. "It's not safe here. We will leave a note for your dad, telling him where to find use."

Back in the car, Lexi and Jack clutched their new guardians with timid trust. They barely spoke as the convoy moved on. When they arrived at the hardware store, the group got to work. Jillian and Ross picked out buckets of paint in bright, warm tones. Derek found a few rolls of family-style prints, landscapes, smiling faces, even cartoon murals. Blankets, curtains, and picture frames followed.

In the gardening section, they struck gold, packets of vegetable and fruit seeds, gloves, spades, watering cans. It was a chance to grow something real. Something that felt like life again.

As they finished loading supplies into an old delivery van they found in the loading bay, Ross somehow got it running, Liam's voice rang out from the rooftop.

"Horde incoming! We need to go, now!"

No time to argue. They threw the last of the bags in the vehicles. Bill helped Lexi and Jack into the car, slamming the door shut just as the first groans echoed down the street. The engines roared to life. Derek behind the wheel of the van, Ross steering the car. They took off, tires screeching, just ahead of the slow-moving swarm. Behind them, the horde poured out into the streets, but the group was already gone, headed back toward the prison. Back toward hope. Back to make a home.

The road stretched quiet and long, the sun beginning to dip below the trees. In the car, Liam drove while Bill sat up front, the kids huddled in the backseat with Ross. Lexi leaned forward between them, her voice soft but curious. "Where are we going?"

Liam glanced in the rear-view mirror, offering her a kind smile. "We're hold up in a prison. It's safe, walls, fences, guard towers, the whole lot." Lexi's eyes widened slightly.

Jack's grip on her arm tightened. "A prison?" he said, his voice small. "Isn't that where bad guys go?"

Bill chuckled lightly. "Normally, yes. But not now. There's no bad guys there, promise. It's just people like us. People trying to survive."

Liam added, "And there's other kids there too. Sophie and Mazie, they're 8 and 10. Then there's Josh, Aaron, James, and Harry. They're all between 5 and 11. You'll get along great."

Lexi exchanged a glance with Jack, and he nodded shyly. "Okay," she said quietly. "That sounds... kind of nice."

"We'll get you settled," Bill said, turning to look at them briefly. "Then we can talk more about your dad. Maybe we can find him." Lexi smiled for the first time. "Thanks."

In the van, the mood was more subdued. Derek's hands gripped the wheel, his eyes fixed on the road ahead. Jillian sat quietly in the passenger seat, looking out the window, her fingers fiddling with the fabric of her sleeve. They made idle small talk, weather, what the prison garden might look like, silly names for paint colours, until the silence stretched just a little too long. Jillian turned to him, her voice soft.

"Derek... Can I tell you something?"

He glanced over, nodding. "Sure."

"I... I like you. More than I should. More than just a brother-in-law or a friend." She paused, breathing in. "I know you're with Jennifer, and I'm not trying to come between that. I just... I needed you to know."

Derek's hands tensed slightly on the steering wheel. He didn't answer right away. Then, gently, he said, "You'll always be special to me, Jillian. You're my sister-in-law. I'll always look out for you. But... you know I'm with Jennifer."

Jillian nodded, brushing her hair behind her ear and blinking fast. "Can I just... hug you? For a bit?"

Derek nodded again. "Yeah... yes, that's okay."

She slid across the bench seat, resting her head on his shoulder, arms around him gently. Derek kept his eyes on the road, but his mind was spinning.

The sun was just beginning to dip behind the treeline as the car and van pulled up to the gate. Jennifer stood there, rifle slung over her shoulder. The second she saw them, her face lit up with relief. She swung the gate open quickly, waving them in. The vehicles rolled into the yard, the weight of the day starting to lift. Supplies had been found. Seeds and paint had been brought back. And two new souls, innocent and full of hope, were coming home.

As the vehicles came to a stop in the prison yard, Derek stepped out of the van, stretching his back and rolling his shoulders after the drive. Jillian exited on the passenger side, her expression unreadable. From the car, Liam, Ross and Bill climbed out, with Lexi and Jack cautiously stepping onto the gravel. Jennifer hurried over to meet them, relief washing over her face.

"You made it back," she said, eyeing the two unfamiliar kids with curiosity.

"We got what we needed," Derek said, giving her a quick kiss. "Paint, tools, gardening stuff... and two new guests." Jennifer raised an eyebrow. "Lexi and Jack," Derek explained. "We found them in a toy store, surviving on sweets and juice. Their dad might still be out there."

Jennifer crouched slightly, offering the kids a warm smile. "You're safe here now, all right? We'll take care of you." The children nodded, both clinging close to each other but already scanning the yard with cautious eyes.

Derek added, "We also picked up some stuff for the kids, games, toys, that sort of thing. We can sort that out soon."

Jennifer nodded, clearly touched. "That'll mean the world to them."

Derek turned to her. "The other group back yet?"

Jennifer shook her head. "Not yet, but they're expected soon."

As if on cue, a dust trail began to rise on the horizon. Jennifer lifted her rifle and peered through the scope, heart pounding.

"It's them!" she called out, a wide smile spreading across her face. "They're back!"

Back on the road, Daryl's team cruised along the quiet roads. The drive home had been thankfully uneventful, no threats, no detours, just the steady hum of tires on tarmac and the occasional nervous glance toward the treeline.

"I can't wait to get back and show them how we did," Sarah said, her tone upbeat. "I bet everyone will be pleased."

Ashley smiled, but her focus was on Stephen, who sat quietly beside her, staring out the window. He hadn't said much. The weight of disappointment sat heavy on him—his hope of finding his children dwindling.

Ashley reached over and gently placed a hand on his arm. "We'll find them," she said softly. "You never know where they might turn up."

Daryl, glancing into the rearview mirror, added, "When we're back, we'll have a proper think about where they could've gone. We'll get a group together and go searching."

Stephen gave a small nod, and for the first time in a while, a faint smile cracked across his tired face. Up front, Callum, now behind the wheel, squinted at the road ahead. Home coming up, he announced. And there it was, the silhouette of the prison rising over the horizon like a fortress. Relief washed over them all.

As they pulled up to the gate, Jennifer was already there, rifle in hand but lowered. She waved them in, smiling with visible relief. Derek stood beside the truck he had just arrived in, arms crossed, waiting. The car rolled past and Callum brought it to a stop. Derek walked over as they climbed out. "Any joy?" he asked.

Callum opened the boot with a smirk. "Well, the boot isn't happy it's full. But yes, we did okay."

A few small chuckles escaped the group, a moment of levity well earned. "We also found someone you know," Callum added, stepping aside.

Stephen emerged from the car, his posture heavy, eyes low. Derek's eyes widened slightly.

"Stephen... I'm glad you're still alive."

"Thanks, Derek," Stephen replied quietly. "Just wish I'd found my kids..." But before he could finish, two small figures darted out from behind the second vehicle.

"Dad!" both voices shouted in unison, Lexi and Jack. Stephen turned, his heart seeming to stop. "Lexi? Jack?!" They ran to him, and he dropped to his knees, arms out wide. They crashed into him in a tangle of limbs, sobbing and laughing and hugging all at once. All three were crying tears of shock, of joy, of love found again. Around them, the group watched, silent and moved. Even the hardest faces had softened. A few wiped away tears of their own. It was a rare moment of pure happiness in a world gone mad.

And as the sun began to dip behind the prison walls, the reunited family, along with the rest of the group, made their way inside. It was starting to feel like a home.

Chapter 21 A New start

It had been a few months since the supply run to Crossford, since Stephen had found his children, and the prison had finally begun to feel like more than just four walls and barbed wire.

Outside, the sun beat down on the courtyard as Reggie, Vicki, and David tended the crops. What started as a few rows of hope had grown into neat lines of green, potatoes, carrots, tomatoes, simple but sustaining. The trio moved between the makeshift garden beds with watering cans and trowels, talking quietly, their routine almost second nature now.

Inside, Maggie and Jennifer worked from a ledger at the rec room-turned-supply depot. Weapons and food were strictly logged, who took what, when, and why. Every bullet counted. Every tin of beans had a name behind it.

Down in the cell blocks, Ashley, Sarah, and Mary were finishing up what had once seemed like an impossible task of making a prison feel like home. The cells were now painted in warm, calming tones. Curtains made from salvaged sheets hung over doorways, softening the harshness of metal bars. A few pictures and posters hung on the walls, smiling faces, peaceful landscapes, children's drawings. The place had changed. It no longer echoed with emptiness and fear. It had life now. Colour. Comfort.

At the top of the main block, Derek stood at the door of the former warden's office. Now repurposed as their main meeting space, the room had a large desk, several mismatched chairs, and a whiteboard scavenged from the nearby school. On it were lists of jobs, supplies, scouting schedules. The kind of order that kept people alive.

He'd called a meeting. As the room filled, Callum, Jennifer, Jillian, Maggie, Bill, Daryl, Anne, and Lee took their seats. These were the ones he trusted most. Survivors, leaders, friends. Once everyone had settled, Derek stood.

"Now that things have calmed," he began, "I want to bring back the council we had at the school. Back then, we made decisions together day-to-day, long term. That's what helped us survive. And that's what we need now." He looked around the room at the faces before him. "All of us, this group, will be the council. We'll guide this place forward."

Daryl leaned back with a grin. "Yeah, but let's not pretend. The big choices still fall to you, our glorious leader, Derek," he said with mock formality.

A round of laughter followed. But even in jest, there was truth to Daryl's words. And everyone in the room knew it. Still, they all nodded in agreement. The prison wasn't just a shelter anymore. It was a home.

"First order of business," Derek said, turning to the whiteboard behind him. The surface was covered with neat writing, names, roles, responsibilities. "Jobs." He stepped aside so everyone in the room could see clearly. "Some of these are already assigned," he continued. "But I want to make sure everyone's still okay with what they've been doing… and that nothing needs changing." He began reading them off:

"Im on supply runs and the council."

"Maggie you on weapons control and the council."

"Jennifer, you're on food control on the council."

"Jillian you're on morale and on the council."

"Callum my second in command, on supply runs also on the council."

"Lee, you're on supply runs and the council."

"Bill your head of security and on the council."

"Daryl, you're our hunter and tracker and the council."

"Anne, you're our teacher for the kids once we get the school room sorted and on the council."

"Father Luke is going to sort out a room to convert to a church."

"Vicki and David are on gardening duties."

"Ashley, Sarah and Mary are on decorating duties"

He paused, then added, "The rest of the adults will rotate between guard duty and perimeter sweeps, just like before."Derek turned to the group. "Are you all okay with this so far?" Around the table, heads nodded in agreement. There were no objections. No hesitation. Everyone knew what they were good at.

What they brought to the group."Good," Derek said with a small smile. "Then we're on the right track."

"Second order of business," Derek said, pacing slowly in front of the whiteboard. "We need to start going further on our supply runs. We've already hit most of the shops within range. It won't take a rocket scientist to figure out we're the centre of all that activity if anyone's watching, we're going to be obvious soon." The room murmured in agreement.

Callum nodded. "We've cleared a lot of ground already. Anything close by has probably been picked clean."

Jennifer leaned forward, her voice steady. "And while we're out there, we should be looking for survivors too. We're safe here, but not everyone's that lucky. If there's a chance to bring people in, we should take it."

Daryl raised an eyebrow. "We could set up an outpost or something. Somewhere to take people first, blindfold them if we need to, until we trust them enough to bring them here." A low rumble of voices quickly filled the room as some agreed and others hesitated.

"That's risky," Bill said flatly. "Could lead the wrong people straight back to us."

"Or we let good people die because we're too cautious," Anne countered.

The debate started heating up but Derek raised his hand. "That's enough for now," he said calmly. "We'll discuss it further, set rules, and figure out protocols.

But the idea's on the table." He waited until the room settled before continuing.

"Third order of business is power. We need to try and get electricity working again. If we can restore power, we can bring the electric gates online. Maybe even get the security cameras going."

"Would be a game changer," Maggie said.

Lee scratched his chin. "Stephen might be our guy. He's from around here he might know where we can find generators or even solar gear."

"Talk to him," Derek said with a nod. "The sooner we figure that out, the better." He turned back to the board, tapped the last item. "Last order of business for now. We need a name. We can't keep calling this place the prison. It doesn't feel right, not anymore. This is our home now. I want everyone to come up with ideas, something we can put to a vote." The council nodded again, the mood shifting from strategy to a quiet sense of pride. They were building something here. Something real.

Outside in the yard, laughter echoed as Stephen played with Lexi and Jack, the two of them beaming as they pushed toy cars through the dirt. The sun had warmed the afternoon, and for a brief moment, it felt like a world without chaos. "Stephen!" Lee called out, approaching from the walkway near the cell block.

Stephen turned, still smiling, and jogged over. "Everything okay?" he asked, brushing dust from his hands.

"Yeah," Lee said. "We're planning a run soon, looking for power sources. Generators, solar panels... anything we can get working. You wouldn't happen to know if there's anywhere nearby that might have that sort of stuff, would you?"

Stephen paused, eyes narrowing in thought. Then, as if a switch had flipped, he nodded. "Yeah... actually, yes. There's a construction site just outside Crossford, in the next village over. They were building a bunch of new houses, and I remember a lot of them were supposed to get solar panels. Not all of them got installed before... well, before everything. But there were diesel generators on site too, temporary ones to power tools and lights."

Lee's face lit up. "Can you show me on the map?"

"Sure," Stephen said. "And please call me Steph. I prefer it."

"Will do, Steph," Lee replied with a grin. The two of them turned and headed inside, the weight of their mission pulling them back into the reality of survival, but with a glimmer of hope. Derek had set up a simple wooden box with a slit in the top, placing it just outside the canteen with a sign above it: Name, Suggestion submitted by Dinner. All council members had been told to write down their suggestions, something hopeful, something better than "the prison." Something that said home.

Later, Lee found Derek near the gate. "Hey, you got a minute?" Lee asked.

"Sure," Derek replied.

Lee unrolled a dog-eared map and pointed just west of Crossford. "Steph reckons this construction site here might have the generators and solar stuff we need. Said they were building a new estate just before it all went down."

Derek nodded. "Alright. Thanks. We'll put together a team and sort out a plan tomorrow. Got a few things I need to take care of tonight."

"Fair enough" Lee said, giving a quick nod before heading off.

Derek made his way toward B Block, searching for Jennifer. He found her alone, humming to herself as she hung a patterned blanket on the wall and straightened a picture frame she'd scavenged. He crept up quietly and grabbed her waist from behind. She shrieked and spun, eyes wide. Instinct took over and she shoved him back hard. Then, seeing his smirk, she let out a breath and gave him a playful slap.

"You scared the life outta me, you idiot."

"Ouch," Derek chuckled, rubbing his arm. "Worth it, though."

He reached into his pocket and pulled out a small silver crucifix. "Found this when Jillian and I were coming to the prison. Thought you might want it."

Jennifer took it, eyes softening as she ran her fingers over it. "It's beautiful," she said quietly. He fastened it around her neck. "I've not really had time for faith," she whispered. "Not since everything went to hell.

But… this? This helps." She kissed him, deeply, and they slipped into one of the nearby cells, once cold and lifeless, now softened with light and warmth, where they made love, comforted by each other and the fragile peace they were building.

Later, the canteen was full, the aroma of stew thick in the air. Everyone had gathered, faces hopeful, some still cautious as Derek stood at the front, the suggestion box in hand. "Right," he said, pulling out slips of paper. "We got a lot of great ideas… and some terrible handwriting." He squinted at the first one. "This says… Preesohn? What?" He shook his head. The second one was worse. "Looks like someone spilled soup on this." The third? Derek held it up, frowned, and without a word, tore it in half. Callum burst out laughing.

"What? You didn't like Zombieville Deluxe?" he said through chuckles.

Derek shot him a look. "Not even a little bit." The group chuckled, the mood lightened. "Alright, here are the four real contenders," Derek said, clearing his throat:

We have New Haven, Sanctuary Hill, Fort Hope and Safehold.

He held the slips up one by one. "We'll put it to a vote tomorrow. For now let's eat, rest, and remember: this place is ours. Let's make it something worth protecting." The crowd clapped softly, some nodding, others whispering among themselves. For the first time in a long while, it felt like they weren't just surviving. They were building something. Something new, and this time, it would last.

Chapter 22: The Vote and the Power

The morning started in the canteen, the smell of porridge and weak coffee in the air. Everyone had cast their votes the night before, and the room buzzed with quiet anticipation. Derek stood at the front, holding a folded piece of paper. "Alright," he began, "the results are in. Out of the five names the council proposed, the one most of you liked..." He paused, unfolding the paper for dramatic effect. "Is New Haven."

A cheer erupted across the room. People clapped, some even whistled. It was the first time in a long time that hope had a name. Ashley stood and clapped her hands.

"Me, Sarah, and Mary can get started painting the new name on the buildings. Give this place some identity."

Derek nodded. "Do it. Big enough to cover the old name, make sure it looks like it's always been New Haven." The positive energy lingered as Derek called the council to the meeting room. Once they were all seated, he got straight to the point. "There's only one thing on the table today," Derek said. "Power. We need it. If we get the electric gates working and the security cameras back online, this place becomes a real fortress."

He continued, "We're going to Glassford, the village after Crossford. There's a construction site nearby, and Steph says there are houses with solar panels and a stash of diesel generators." The council nodded thoughtfully. "The team will be me, Callum, Daryl, Lee, and Steph, "We'll take the truck so we can haul back whatever we find."

"What about backup?" Bill asked.

"We'll have a team ready to come out looking for us if we don't come back in a few days.," Derek replied. "But this is a stealth run. In and out, quiet and quick." The meeting ended with a renewed sense of purpose. New Haven wasn't just a name, it was a promise.

The team loaded up the modified truck, its cab now refitted to seat six comfortably. They packed supplies: fuel, weapons, tools, and a few tarps in case the solar panels needed to be covered. The morning sun rose over New Haven, its new name already stenciled in large, clean lettering on the outer wall of the prison, enough to finally conceal the word that once screamed "PRISON" to anyone who approached. Derek gave Jennifer a tight hug, whispering in her ear, "We'll be back soon. Keep things running."

"You better," she whispered back before pulling him in for a kiss.

Nearby, Callum kissed Anne's forehead and gave her hand a reassuring squeeze. "Stay safe," he said.

"You too," Anne replied, trying not to show her worry. Just as the team turned to leave,

Jillian approached, arms crossed. "Derek, can I come? I haven't had much to do lately. People are happy. I want to help more."

Derek gave her a sympathetic look. "Not this time, Jill. We've got what we need, and it might get messy. Next one, I promise."

She scowled, spinning on her heel and marching off. Jennifer, noticing the hurt in her expression, sighed and followed after her.

Derek turned toward the gate. "Liam! Open it up!" The heavy doors groaned as they swung open. With a final wave, the truck rolled out onto the road. The gate slammed shut behind them with a thud that echoed against the prison walls. Unbeknownst to them, as the truck rumbled away from New Haven, a figure crouched low in the back, hidden under a tarp. Someone had hitched a ride.

But who it was they wouldn't know until they reached Glassford.

The drive was calm. The countryside was eerily quiet, fields overgrown, nature slowly reclaiming the roads. The hum of the truck's engine was the only constant sound, and the occasional buzz of static on the radio. Callum, sitting shotgun, scanned the map. "About five minutes out. Should see the rooftops soon."

In the back, Steph kept his eyes on the road behind, more out of habit than concern. Daryl and Lee quietly checked over their gear. No one spoke much, the tension of every run still hung heavy, no matter how peaceful the road seemed.

As they crested a hill, the remnants of the village of Glassford came into view. Rows of half-finished houses sat like skeletons in the distance. Some looked untouched, while others had caved-in roofs or scorched walls. A massive construction site sprawled to the north, dotted with machinery and storage units.

"That's the one," Steph pointed. "They were starting a whole new development here. Solar panels were going on the upper rows, and they had diesel generators in storage for site power."

Derek nodded and slowed the truck, parking behind a low hedge out of direct sight. The team disembarked, each instinctively checking their surroundings, weapons drawn. "Daryl," Derek said, "you and Lee scout the area. Make sure no surprises are waiting. Steph and Callum, we'll head to the storage units. I'll check the houses for panels we can remove." Just as they were about to split, a sound stopped them. A rustling from the truck. The tarp in the back shifted. Weapons instantly raised, tense fingers resting on triggers.

"Come out," Derek ordered, "slow and hands up!" The tarp was flung aside, and out crawled Jillian. Everyone stared in disbelief. "You've got to be kidding me," Derek said through clenched teeth.

"I told you I needed to help!" Jillian snapped, her voice defiant but laced with guilt. "I couldn't just sit there while you all went out again."

Daryl let out a groan. "You're lucky we didn't shoot you on reflex."

Derek rubbed his face in frustration. "We'll deal with this later. You stay close. And silent. One wrong move and you're going back with an escort." Jillian nodded, chastened but unrepentant. "Alright," Derek said, refocusing, "let's get to work." The teams moved out, the quiet ruins of Glassford waiting for them along with whatever dangers might still lurk in the shells of its unfinished dreams.

The teams had split up but slightly differently as planned this time. Derek, Callum, and Jillian worked their way toward the construction site's storage containers, aiming to find the diesel generators Steph had told them about. Meanwhile, Daryl, Lee, and Steph moved toward the line of new-build houses, hoping to salvage intact solar panels.

At the containers, Derek gave Jillian a quick nod as she passed him a pry bar. "Alright, let's get into this thing fast. Eyes sharp." Callum jammed the bar into the heavy lock on the first container. With a grunt and a pop, it snapped free and the rusted doors creaked open. Inside were two large generators, covered in dust but seemingly untouched by looters.

"There they are," Callum said. "Steph was right."

Derek stepped inside carefully. "We'll need to rig a way to load these onto the truck. Jillian, check around for a lift or anything we can use to wheel them." Jillian nodded, already scanning the area. A few minutes later, she returned with an old but sturdy trolley jack.

"Found this by the site office. Think we can make it work?"

Derek smiled. "You're getting good at this." She blushed slightly but said nothing, helping to guide the jack into place.

Meanwhile, on the far side of the site, Steph stood alongside Daryl and Lee, all three looking up at a row of new homes. Some of the solar panels had been ripped off by weather or time, but others were still firmly in place. Steph pointed to a house at the end. "That row's your best bet. Panels are newer. I remember they were just finishing installation when... well, when everything fell apart."

Lee nodded. "Let's make this quick."

As they moved into position, Daryl kept watch. Steph and Lee started up the scaffolding carefully, dismantling the panels with hand tools. But then came the sound. Low, guttural groaning. Daryl swung his crossbow around, eyes narrowing. "We've got movement on the north end of the site." From behind the partially built walls and scattered building equipment, zombies began to appear. Slow, stumbling, but numerous. Daryl raised his radio. "Derek, you've got company."

Back at the containers, Derek's radio crackled to life. He cursed under his breath. "Jillian, Callum, load the first generator now. I'll cover." Jillian dropped to one knee, helping guide the jack with Callum while Derek moved to the entrance, rifle raised. "Let's be quick about this, ok." he demands.

Callum smirked. "Always are."

Over by the houses, Daryl whispered, "No gunfire unless we have to, keep it clean." He moved ahead, blade out, taking down two zombies that had gotten too close. Lee and Steph worked faster, lowering the last of the intact panels. Steph grimaced. "There isn't going to be enough time…"

"Fall back to the truck! Now!" Daryl barked. Back at the truck, the first generator was already half-lifted onto the truck's flatbed. Jillian looked up, breathing heavily.

"We need five more minutes."

"You've got three," Derek replied. "Move." As the two groups converged at the truck, the zombies came closer, dozens of them, their groans rising over the collapsing silence of the abandoned site.

As the group scrambled to load the second generator, Derek caught sight of a new threat, shadows moving fast from the opposite end of the site. "More incoming! Front of the truck!" he shouted. Sure enough, another twenty zombies shambled into view from the main road, their sunken eyes locked onto the sound of the struggle. The group was boxed in. "Leave the truck!" Derek yelled. "Everyone head to the scaffolding!"

Without hesitation, the team abandoned their cargo. Daryl fired a few cover shots as Callum, Jillian, and Steph made a break for the metal staircase that snaked up the scaffolding. Derek stayed at the rear, watching the numbers swell. Lee and Steph ran side by side, trying to catch up, when a chunk of broken concrete sent them both tumbling hard to the ground.

"Get up!" Daryl barked, already turning back but he could see the look in Lee's eyes. Steph grabbed Lee's arm and they scrambled up, but the horde was almost on them. Derek turned to help, but Steph shouted, "Go!" The container doors just ahead of them had been left open. Lee and Steph made a split-second decision. Together, they dove inside and yanked the heavy metal doors shut just as the first wave of zombies slammed into them. Inside, it was pitch black.

Outside, dozens of zombies smashed against the doors, but by some stroke of luck or fate the force slammed the lock catch into place. It clicked shut, sealing them in. Trapped, but alive. On the scaffolding, Derek and the others reached the rooftop. He looked down to see the truck swarmed, the metal container surrounded. He cursed under his breath. "Steph and Lee are in that box."

Jillian looked pale. "Are they—"

"Alive," Derek cut her off. "But stuck." The rooftop gave a full view of the carnage below, about sixty or more zombies now roamed the construction site. The truck was lost, their supplies gone, and two of their own were locked in a box surrounded by the dead.

"We need a plan," Callum said, panting. "We can't leave them in there."

Daryl crouched low, watching the herd. "We'll wait it out. They'll wander eventually.. they always do."

Derek nodded, though the knot in his chest was tightening. "We wait. And then we go back for them. We're not leaving anyone behind."

The group huddled close on the roof as the sun began to lower in the sky, the groans of the undead echoing through the broken skeletons of homes. A few hours passed. The sun was beginning to dip toward the horizon, casting a golden haze over the half-built houses and steel beams. From their perch on the roof, the group watched the horde. Only a handful, maybe ten had wandered off after a lone deer had wandered too close to the site.

Most of the undead remained, aimlessly circling the truck and the container where Lee and Steph were still trapped. Daryl scanned the nearby buildings, eyes darting across broken windows and empty frames. "There," he muttered.

"What is it?" Callum asked, joining him.

Daryl pointed to the upper floor of the third house down. "Glass bottles and jerry cans. Bingo."

With Callum's help, Daryl quickly descended the scaffolding, made his way inside, grabbed what he needed, and was back up before the herd noticed. As late afternoon settled in, the worry for Lee and Steph was growing. Derek noticed Daryl and Callum laying out supplies. They were tearing fabric into strips, soaking them in the fuel.

"Molotovs?" he asked.

"Only way," Daryl replied, pulling out the old lighter he'd kept since the early days. "Let's clear a path."

Derek nodded in approval. "Good thinking." They prepped nine makeshift bombs, Daryl and Derek even sacrificing their shirt sleeves for the cause. Daryl lit the first one, and Callum hurled it toward the container. The flames exploded across the crowd of undead, engulfing several instantly. Two more followed, igniting the remaining zombies around the container in a fiery blaze. Screeches filled the air as burning zombies collapsed in heaps. Next, the remaining undead at the base of the scaffolding. Three more bombs. Three more eruptions. The fire cleansed the site in heat and chaos.

As the final flames died down, only five undead remained trapped inside one of the buildings. Derek and Daryl descended quietly, their knives ready. One by one, they cleared the last threats. The fight was over. Derek jogged over to the container and yanked the lock. The doors creaked open, light spilling in. Lee and Steph squinted as their eyes adjusted.

"Outside and on the ground!" Callum barked in a mock-serious tone. They stepped out blinking, and Callum burst into laughter. "Had to," he grinned.

"Ha ha," Lee muttered, shaking his head. "You're hilarious."

Derek didn't waste time. "Alright. Load up. Fast. We're not pushing our luck again." As the team began hauling supplies to the truck, Jillian disappeared inside the construction site's office. As the last of the solar panels was loaded and the sun neared the horizon, Derek looked around. "Jillian?" he called. He found her back in the office, standing beside a cooler.

"I'm sorry," she said quietly. "For sneaking in the truck. I just.. I thought I might die without ever doing something that mattered."

"It was daft," Derek said, sighing. "But.. you helped. A lot." He reached into his pocket and pulled out the charm bracelet from the treehouse. Gently, he fastened it around her wrist.

"It's beautiful," she whispered.

"I was going to give it to you when we got back. Belated birthday gift." She smiled and threw her arms around him. He hugged her back. As they pulled away, their eyes locked and Jillian kissed him. Derek froze.

"Derek!" a voice echoed. Daryl, heading their way. They pulled apart quickly. "Just coming!" Derek shouted back. He grabbed the cooler and turned toward the door. Jillian followed, clutching the first aid kits she had found.

"There use are," Daryl said, sounding impatient. "We need to go before more of those freaks show up."

They loaded the final supplies, solar panels, generators, water and fuel into the back of the truck. As the engine rumbled to life and the sun dipped below the treetops, the truck pulled away from Glassford, heading back toward New Haven. A successful mission. A close call. And a secret kiss that could change everything.

Chapter 23 – Homecomings and Secrets

The truck rumbled down the empty backroads as the last light of day faded into the shadows of the trees. The hum of the engine was the only sound for miles, an oddly calming contrast to the chaos they'd just left behind. Everyone in the truck was quiet, lost in their own thoughts. Lee and Steph sat silently near the back, still processing their near-death experience inside the container. Callum, riding shotgun, kept his eyes on the tree line, ever alert for any sign of movement. Derek sat at the wheel, hands gripping the steering tightly not from fear, but from the weight of what had happened...and what had almost happened.

Jillian sat in the middle, her head gently leaning against the window, fingers absently touching the charm bracelet on her wrist. She hadn't said a word since they left Glassford, but she kept stealing glances at Derek, who deliberately kept his focus on the road ahead. As they passed a burned-out petrol station,

Daryl finally broke the silence. "We got damn lucky back there."

Callum nodded. "Yeah. If that container door hadn't held..."

"But it did," Derek said firmly. "And we're going home. That's all that matters."

As if on cue, the silhouette of the prison, New Haven, appeared over the horizon. The sight triggered a wave of relief among the group. Safety. Familiar faces. Rest. When they reached the front gate, Liam was already there, rifle slung over his shoulder. He signaled to the towers, and the gates creaked open. The truck rolled in, greeted by a small crowd of people gathered in the courtyard. Jennifer among them. As soon as the truck stopped, she rushed forward to greet Derek, arms wrapping tightly around his neck. "You're back," she said, her voice filled with relief.

He nodded and kissed her cheek. "We got everything. Panels, generators, some fuel, water… Even a few medical supplies."

Callum found Anne and hugged her tightly while the others jumped down and began unloading the truck. Steph was immediately pulled into a hug by Father Luke, and even Ashley and Sarah came running to ask questions and offer help. As the supplies were carted away, Derek caught sight of Jillian lingering by the truck, her expression unreadable.

"You all right?" he asked as he approached her.

She nodded. "Yeah. Just tired."

"You did good today," he said softly. Before she could reply, Jennifer called out,

"Derek! We need to decide where we're storing the panels." He turned to Jillian one last time.

"Later?"

Jillian gave a faint smile. "Later."

And with that, the team split to help organize the supplies, their return celebrated quietly but with deep gratitude. In the midst of an unforgiving world, New Haven had grown stronger. But even as the community thrived, small cracks were beginning to show beneath the surface, cracks formed by close calls, buried feelings, and secrets left unspoken.

The next morning, the sun was barely over the horizon when Derek, Callum, Lee, Daryl, Steph, and a few others climbed onto the roof of the main admin block. The solar panels, now unboxed and ready, lay stacked neatly beside them. Each one was heavier than expected, and with every trip up the ladder, the strain grew worse. Jillian handed up tools and cables from the ground, her energy surprisingly fresh despite the events of the day before. Derek gave her a thankful nod as he wiped sweat from his brow.

"Let's make this place shine," Steph said, kneeling beside Lee as they began following the faded instruction booklet they'd found with the panels. One by one, the panels were mounted and fixed into place. The cables were run neatly down the roof, along the gutters, and into the battery storage room they'd cleared out the night before. The batteries, though old, were clean and looked mostly unused. But wiring them to the power grid of the prison, now that was another matter entirely.

The group crouched in the power room, wires spread everywhere like a spaghetti bowl of uncertainty. None of them were electricians. Trial and error was the name of the game. After two hours of fiddling, plugging, unplugging, arguing, and a few unfortunate shocks, mostly to Callum, they finally heard a faint hum.

The lights flickered. Everyone froze. Then a buzz! The room filled with light. Down the hall, more lights came to life one by one. The sound of motors hummed to life as the electric gates groaned into movement. A low whir signaled the return of life to the camera systems. Cheers erupted from the group. Daryl clapped Lee on the back. Jillian let out a whoop from the hallway. Callum slumped against the wall, laughing between breaths.

"We did it," Derek said, exhausted but grinning. "New Haven's got power." At the security room, Bill spun in his chair as the monitors blinked to life, one after another.

"Yes!" he shouted, punching the air. "I can see everything!" Rows of screens now showed almost every corner of the facility. Courtyards, corridors, the walls, the gates. Everything except the showers and bathrooms, of course. Derek entered moments later, still catching his breath.

"All of them working?" he asked.

Bill nodded, practically glowing with pride. "All but the private areas. Got a view of the gates, all blocks, storage, and the rec yard."

Derek folded his arms, thinking. "What about the cameras inside the cells? Should we leave those on?"

Bill hesitated. "Could be a breach of privacy."

"Yeah," Derek agreed. "Take it to the council later. For now, keep them running, just in case."

By late afternoon, the team that installed the panels had finally cleaned up and gotten a chance to rest. Some lay sprawled in the grass outside the canteen, others sat on the steps of B Block, sipping from metal cups of cool water. The mood in New Haven was the best it had been since the outbreak began.

Children chased each other with sticks, laughter echoing off the stone walls. Ashley, Mary, and Sarah hung up colorful drawings and curtains they'd been working on for the communal areas. Maggie was teaching one of the newcomers how to clean and store rifles. Even Father Luke had gathered a small group in the chapel for quiet reflection.

Jillian walked through the courtyard and smiled. For the first time in a long time, things didn't feel temporary. They felt like home. Derek stood with Jennifer by the gate, arms loosely around her as they watched the sunset together. New Haven wasn't just surviving anymore. It was living. The evening air in New Haven was cool and still. The lights from the newly powered floodlamps cast soft pools of brightness around the courtyard, illuminating the high walls and creating long shadows between buildings. The hum of energy, subtle but present, served as a reminder of the progress they had made.

In the meeting room, once the warden's office, Derek sat at the head of the long table, a cup of lukewarm tea in hand. The other council members were slowly trickling in: Maggie, Jennifer, Jillian, Callum, Lee, Daryl, Bill, and Anne. As the last of them took their seats, Derek cleared his throat. "Appreciate you all for being here tonight. I know we're shattered after

today. But there's one thing we need to settle."
Everyone looked his way, silent and attentive.

"The cameras inside the cells," Derek said. "I know
they were part of the old system, but we're not prison
guards. People have been through enough without
feeling like they're being watched in what's supposed
to be their private space."

Bill rubbed his chin, then nodded slowly. "I get it.
Security-wise, they're helpful. But yes... we're not
running a jail. We're building a community."

"There's already cameras everywhere else," Jennifer
added. "Gates, corridors, yards. If someone's up to
something shady, we'll see it. But people deserve
somewhere that feels like theirs."

Callum leaned back in his chair. "It's like Big Brother,
you know? All-seeing eye. I wouldn't want a camera
pointed at my bunk every time I close my eyes."

Anne gave a small smile. "I've been teaching the kids
about privacy and boundaries. Hard to reinforce that
when cameras are watching them sleep."

The group fell into a short debate, mostly around
safety versus trust, but by the end of it, the consensus
was clear.

Derek leaned forward. "Alright, then. We switch off
the cell cameras. Leave the rest active. If anyone asks,
we tell them the truth, we trust them, and we believe
people need their own space." Everyone nodded in
agreement.

Derek let out a breath and slumped back in his chair, exhaustion settling into his bones. The adrenaline of the day had faded. His muscles ached, his eyes burned, and his mind was barely keeping up. "I'm knackered," he muttered, earning a round of quiet chuckles.

"Join the club," Maggie said.

"One day without drama would be nice," Lee added.

Jillian stood and stretched. "Still... It's been a good day. For once."

Derek gave a tired but genuine smile. "Yeah. It really has."

As the council dispersed, each heading back to their quarters, Derek lingered for a few more minutes, staring at the flickering light on the far wall. New Haven was growing, stronger, safer. But with every step forward came new challenges, new questions. He knew peace wouldn't last forever. But tonight? It was enough. And for the first time in a long time...

...it felt like hope.

Derek was the last to leave, but as he walked out, Jillian was waiting to talk to him. "It's later now, Derek," she says.

"You're right we need to discuss things." "Give me 15 minutes and meet me in A-block," he replied, knowing it was empty for now. She nodded and left.

Derek made his way to the security office to see how Bill was, but he was buzzing with excitement. He had switched off all the internal cameras bar the main lobby for the night, but left all the external ones active. Derek tells him to mind switch out with someone and get some rest. Also, to get some extra people on security.

Bill replied, "I've already got Steph and Ross on board." He gave a thumbs-up to Derek before Derek left. Derek went into B-block to see Jennifer, but by this time only Lily and Father Luke were still awake, both turning in for the night. Derek headed up to the faraway cell which was his and Jennifer's. She was sound asleep by now but stirred slightly, just enough to give him a kiss before drifting back off. After 10 minutes, he got up and headed to A-block.

A-block was quiet, the stillness wrapping around the empty cell block like a blanket. The faint hum of the restored power vibrated through the walls, a strange comfort after so many months in the dark. Derek stepped inside and found Jillian already waiting near the far end, sitting on a makeshift bench against the wall. Her arms were folded tightly, knees bouncing with nervous energy. She glanced up as he approached, offering a faint smile that didn't quite reach her eyes.

"You came," she said softly.

"You asked," he replied, leaning against the opposite wall. "Figured it's time we talk properly."

Jillian nodded, her eyes drifting toward the floor. "Look, I want to say sorry for earlier. For sneaking on the truck. For... what happened at the site."

Derek exhaled, keeping his tone calm. "It was reckless. But yes, you helped. We needed every pair of hands we could get." He paused. "As for what happened between us…"

She cut in. "I know you're with Jennifer. I wasn't trying to steal you away or ruin something. I just… I acted on something. Something real. At least, it was for me."

Derek's jaw tightened. "You think I don't feel things too? Jill, I'm not made of stone."

"Then why did you pull away?" she snapped, stepping toward him now. "Why do you keep acting like what happened didn't mean something?"

"Because it can't," he shot back, keeping his voice low but firm. "This, us, whatever that was… it's not simple. I've got someone. Someone who's stood by me through all this."

"And I haven't?" Her voice cracked with frustration. "I've fought, I've worked, I've bled beside you. You think I don't lie awake at night thinking about how close we all are to losing each other? Thinking about you?" Derek looked away, jaw clenched. Jillian stepped closer. "You kissed me too. Don't stand there and pretend that didn't happen. Don't treat it like some mistake you're trying to bury."

Derek stood frozen, caught between guilt and confusion, but before he could speak, Jillian's voice broke. "I love you, Derek," she said, almost in a whisper. "I know you're with Jennifer, and I don't want to ruin that. But I lie in bed at night and I hear you two... laughing, talking, even when you think no one else can hear. And all I can do is wish it was me instead of her." Her voice cracked, tears now streaming freely. "I didn't want this to happen. I didn't mean for it to. But I love you. And I've been carrying that around every damn day like it's a sin." Overwhelmed, she dropped to her knees, sobbing quietly into her hands.

Derek's breath caught in his chest. For a long moment he just stood there, staring at her broken form. Then, slowly, he stepped forward and dropped to one knee. He gently pulled her into a hug, wrapping his arms around her as she wept into his shoulder, her entire body trembling. Neither spoke. The only sound in A-block was the soft hum of power and the quiet heartbreak of something unspoken too long.

After a few quiet moments, Jillian slowly lifted her head, her cheeks still streaked with tears. Derek looked at her, his expression unreadable, then gently raised a hand to her face. As he went to wipe away the tears, she leaned into his palm, her eyes closing briefly before locking with his.

There was a beat, heavy, electric, silent. Then they kissed. This time, there was no hesitation. No second thoughts. Just raw emotion and months of buried tension exploding to the surface. Their hands fumbled as they clung to each other, pulling closer, deeper. They sank to the floor, the kiss growing hungrier by the second. Derek paused, breathless, eyes searching hers. Jillian simply nodded. They stood quickly, stripping off clothes in a flurry of urgency and need, before stumbling into the nearest cell. The cold concrete and steel bars faded away as they collapsed into each other, lost in the heat of the moment. For that night, there was no war outside, no undead world. Just them.

They spent the rest of the night making love, not speaking, not thinking, just feeling.

Chapter 24: Old Foes

At New Haven, morning light crept through the reinforced windows of A-block. Derek stirred, his body sore, his mind clouded. As he blinked against the sun, the first thing he thought was that he wasn't in his usual cell, and he wasn't alone. Except.. he was. Jillian was gone. Only his boxers remained, barely covering his modesty. He sat up slowly, rubbing his face. The memories of the night before surged through his mind, sharp and vivid. Guilt hit him like a hammer. He quickly got dressed, running a hand through his messy hair and stepping out of the cell.

As he exited A-block, Jennifer's voice called out with relief, "There you are! I've been looking for you." Without hesitation, she walked up and gave him a kiss. "Good morning." Still shaking the cobwebs from his mind, Derek kissed her back, the weight of what he'd done bearing down heavily. Jennifer continued, cheerful, "The council met this morning, but no one could find you. What happened to you?"

"I'm not entirely sure, to be honest," Derek replied, forcing a shrug. "I must've gotten up during the night and wandered into A-block."

Jennifer chuckled, giving him a playful slap on the arm. "Just make sure you don't start wandering into other cells and think they're me."

Derek mustered a faint smile, trying to match her lightness, but inside he was a mess. As Jennifer walked away down the corridor, he watched her go, guilt twisting deeper in his chest. He knew what he had to do. He had to find Jillian. They needed to talk. Derek scanned the yard, searching until he spotted her near the vegetable garden. He walked toward her, slow but determined.

"Hi Derek," she greeted him with a smile as he approached.

"Hi Jillian.. can we speak?" "Yeah, sure," she said, wiping her hands and walking with him to a quieter area of the yard. Just as Derek was ready to speak, Jillian beat him to it. "Listen, Derek, I'm really sorry about the other day, for hiding in the back of the truck, and then what happened in the site office with the kiss. As much as I wanted it to happen, afterwards I felt terrible. I saw it in your eyes, you felt it too. I know we were meant to talk last night, but I couldn't face it. I was scared we'd fall out, and I didn't want to risk that. I'm so sorry and I hope we can still be really good friends."

Derek, now utterly confused, replied, "Yeah.. but what about what happened last night?"

Jillian's face showed even more regret. "I'm sorry for not showing up. I really wanted to, but I just.. couldn't do it. I didn't want to take the chance of ruining what we have." She gave him a hug and said softly, "I'll see you later."

Derek stood frozen, his mind racing. Had he dreamt what had happened? It felt so real, but Jillian claimed she never showed up. His thoughts were interrupted by the alarm bell ringing. Callum's voice rang out from the tower.

"The gate! Quick, Derek, come to the gate!" Derek sprinted up the ladder to the watchtower. He reached the top and looked out over the wall. All he could say was,

"Oh no.. you again."

A few months previously at Kinross. Bellamy has been meticulously searching the school and surrounding area at Ellis's behest for any sign of Derek and his group, but nothing. Back in Kinross, he tells Ellis they've been searching for weeks and found no sign of them.

"I think it's safe to say they are dead," Bellamy says.

Ellis stands up from his chair. "Maybe," he replies cryptically. Bellamy still can't get over what he has seen with the zombies and Ellis. To think, if he can control them, what is his end game? Is he going to use them against anyone who doesn't agree with him or fall to his wishes? As Bellamy walks his rounds, a hooded man bumps into him. Instinctively, Bellamy grabs his knife and swings around, but the man is gone. In his hand, a note has been placed. He slips into a small shed and reads it:

"Meet us at 11pm. Railway bridge" The note is signed with a single letter: S. Bellamy sets the note on fire and leaves the shed. Later that night, he slips out of Kinross through a secret door that only a handful know about. He moves through the trees under the cover of darkness, taking long strides, careful not to make noise. The railway bridge comes into view, shrouded in mist and moonlight. The air is thick with tension. Bellamy slows, listening for movement.

"You came, Bellamy."

Bellamy lifts his pistol. "Who's there?" Four figures emerge from the shadows, it's the same group of scientists he had met once before, their faces grim but familiar in the moonlight.

"I assume you've seen them, then," Marcus says.

Bellamy nods slowly, lowering his weapon just slightly. "Yes. I have."

"You've seen nothing yet," George adds, stepping forward.

Marcus continues, "Kinross is just the tip. Ellis isn't keeping his entire operation there." George leans in, his voice lower. "There's a town north of here. Rose Bank. You know it?"

Bellamy nods. "Yeah, I've passed through it."

"There's an old tech facility on the outskirts," Marcus says. "Looks like an abandoned distribution hub from the outside. But it's not."

"It's a lab," George finishes. "Bigger than the one at Kinross. Ellis has moved most of his resources there, the creatures, the data, everything. There's nearly a hundred of those things kept there now. Sedated. Caged. Watched over by another team of scientists. Not like us."

Bellamy's jaw tightens. "What are they doing?"

"Trying to finish what Ellis started," Marcus answers. "Full control. Not just obedience. He wants to command them like soldiers, turn them on whoever refuses to kneel. Entire communities if needed." Bellamy shakes his head. "He's insane."

"He's worse than insane," George snaps. "He's methodical. He believes he's creating a new world order. And with the power to command the dead, who's going to stop him?"

Marcus steps closer. "That's why we reached out to you. We're not part of this anymore. We're done being pawns. And we need your help to expose him. To stop him."

Bellamy glances toward the darkness behind him, then back at the scientists. His mind races. "I need proof," he says. "And if I'm going to move on Ellis, I need allies."

"You'll have them," Marcus replies. "But first.. you need to see Rose Bank for yourself."

Marcus continues, his voice low and urgent. "Rose Bank is the biggest of them all. State-of-the-art labs, generators, reinforced holding cells, a full research wing. It's where most of the funding went. There are another three labs, but Rose Bank.. it's the furthest along in the research."

Bellamy narrowed his eyes. "What kind of research?"

"Complete control," George cut in. "Mental suppression, signal-based commands, herd direction, all of it. They've made progress there that even we never saw."

Marcus stepped forward, more intense now. "Get a team. Find an excuse, anything. But go see it for yourself. You need to witness what he's building before it's too late."

"But we're warning you," George added, his voice grave. "The ones in Rose Bank... they're not like the others. They're smarter. More coordinated. More violent. If you get the chance.. we highly advise you wipe them out."

Bellamy's jaw clenched. "Where are the other three?"

Harold, who had been quiet until now, reached into his jacket and unfolded a hand-drawn map. "Here," he said, pressing it into Bellamy's hands. "We've marked the locations." Bellamy's eyes scanned the paper, his heart starting to race. "One's near Tannochside," Harold explained, "in an old biscuit factory. Ellis bought it under a shell company before the fall."

"The second's to the east near Burnside," Marcus added, "disguised as a community gym called Brave Heart. From the outside, it still looks like a local fitness center."

Bellamy moved his finger to the final mark. "And this one?"

George's expression darkened. "That's the worst of them. South, near the old Kintyre settlement." He paused before continuing.

"It was supposed to be a controlled test. A live trial. Something went wrong. The containment failed, and the infected... they got out. The entire community, over 300 people gone. Slaughtered. And there were over a hundred infected in the lab when it started."

Bellamy went silent, the weight of the information settling hard in his chest. The wind shifted around them, cold and eerie beneath the bridge. He folded the map carefully and tucked it inside his jacket.

"This changes everything," he said.

Marcus nodded. "Then be ready. Because it's only just begun."

Just as Bellamy turned to head back toward Kinross, the sound of the alarm tore through the night air, sharp, shrill, and urgent.

His heart dropped.

Without a second thought, he broke into a sprint, boots pounding against the cracked earth, the map crumpled tightly in his fist. The cold night air whipped past him as he tore through the darkened countryside, the wailing siren getting louder with every step. By the time he reached the outer gate of Kinross, his chest was heaving, and sweat ran down his brow despite the chill. Chaos echoed through the compound, shouting, gunfire, and more alarms. Munroe met him near the main square, rifle in hand.

"Zombies inside the walls," Munroe shouted over the blare. "At least ten, maybe more!"

Bellamy didn't hesitate. "Get the team. Lock down the perimeter. Nothing gets in or out." His voice cut through the panic like a blade. Moments later, his team was moving, armed and fast, sweeping through the narrow streets and alleys of Kinross. The red warning lights cast long shadows across buildings as they cleared one corner after another.

Every turn brought more danger. Zombies shambled from behind fences, out of half-open doors, from the darkness between buildings. The team moved methodically, coordinated shots, axes cracking skulls, boots slamming doors shut behind them. Street by street, the compound was reclaimed.

Finally, Ortega shouted from the courtyard, "Clear! All clear!" Bellamy jogged over, blood streaked across his sleeves. Ortega was counting bodies. "Thirty-four," he confirmed grimly. "Some are ours.. but the rest are the undead."

Raven stepped forward, her face pale under the harsh lights. "How the hell did they get in?"

Bellamy's eyes scanned the blood-smeared yard, his jaw tight. "I don't know," he said, voice low. "But I'll find out." Bellamy's face twisted in fury as he turned sharply. "Ortega, Raven, secure the perimeter. I want to know exactly where they got in, if they even got in at all." Both nodded and took off at a jog, shouting orders as they disappeared into the fading red glow of the emergency lights. "Munroe!" Bellamy barked.

"Take George and Peter. Go house to house, every room, every shed. Make damn sure there's no zombies still moving."

"Yes, sir!" Munroe replied, already moving. Bellamy didn't wait. His blood was boiling. He had a gut feeling, and it was leading him underground. He made his way to the hidden lift, the secret elevator buried beneath the old records room. Swiping his keycard, the doors opened with a hiss. He descended in silence, jaw clenched, hands balled into fists.

The lab was dim when he arrived, the smell of burnt flesh and antiseptic filling the air. There, standing over blood-soaked operating tables and the mutilated remains of Dr. Mirak's team was Ellis, calm, hands folded behind his back. "What a waste," Ellis muttered, surveying the carnage.

Bellamy's voice was cold and sharp. "What happened?"

Ellis turned slowly, expression unreadable. "A test," he said. "A new batch. ZF-16s, obedient, understanding, controlled. All ten of them. They were perfect." He walked slowly across the lab, kicking aside a blood-smeared clipboard. "Until a power surge triggered the emergency alarms. The noise agitated them. They went feral. Attacked Mirak and his team.. killed every last one." Ellis looked down at one of the mangled bodies, expression blank. "The lift opened and they went in. One of them stumbled into the panel and up they went."

Bellamy was on him in an instant. He grabbed Ellis by the collar and slammed him against the wall. "Up they went?" Bellamy roared. "They killed 22 people! My people! How the hell am I supposed to explain that when my men find no breach in the damn perimeter?"

Ellis didn't flinch. "They're prototypes, Bellamy. There will be setbacks."

Bellamy's eyes burned with rage. "Setbacks don't kill innocent people."

I'd advise you to let me go," Ellis said, voice low as Bellamy's grip on Ellis's collar tightened as his teeth ground together. Bellamy held for a moment longer, nostrils flaring, before shoving him back and turning away.

"I'm going topside to secure Kinross," he growled. "You can clean up your own damn mess." Without waiting for a reply, he stormed out, fists clenched and shoulders tense. As he exited the old records room, Ortega and Raven were waiting at the door.

"No breaches, sir," Ortega reported, sweat still beading his brow. He was wiry, his hands never quite still, but his dark eyes stayed fixed and earnest. "We've checked the walls, towers, gates—there's no sign they got in from outside."

Bellamy swore under his breath. "Get Munroe. Have him meet us at command. We're locking Kinross down until further notice. I want the place sealed tight." The two nodded and rushed off. Bellamy stood in the corridor for a moment, letting the tension settle in his chest as he surveyed the aftermath. Bloodied stretchers were still being dragged out. The dead, friends, colleagues, civilians, were being wrapped in sheets. I could kill him, Bellamy thought bitterly. Ellis. The man was dangerous, reckless, deluded. And yet.. still in charge.

A few hours passed. Slowly, Kinross returned to a fragile sense of order. Bodies were incinerated. A wall of flowers and candles formed outside the mess hall as the community mourned. Back in Ellis's office, the man himself sat calmly at his desk, reading something on an old tablet. He didn't even look up as Bellamy entered.

"It's done," Bellamy said quietly. "I convinced my men the zombies got in. Told them there must've been a hidden breach. Munroe created one on the north side just deep enough for them to 'find.' He didn't ask questions."

"Good," Ellis said, still not looking up. "I want you on a run."

Bellamy's expression hardened. "What kind of run?"

"I need fresh test subjects," Ellis said plainly, as if he were asking for supplies. "Bring them back alive. Store them in the old police station cells downtown."

Bellamy's jaw tightened. "Where exactly do I find 'test subjects?'"

Ellis finally looked up, cold and emotionless. "Find people. People who have not turned."

Bellamy, stunned, took a step back. "People?" he said, his voice low, almost disbelieving.

Ellis nodded without a flicker of emotion. "Yes. Now go."

Bellamy clenched his jaw, forcing down the surge of anger and disgust rising in his gut. He turned sharply and left the room, boots heavy against the floor. His team was already gathered in his office, weapons cleaned, gear packed, waiting for orders. They had overheard just enough. Bellamy could feel their eyes on him, searching his face for answers.

He didn't flinch. "Change of plan," he said, voice firm. "Ellis believes the breach came from outside. Says a group of runaways might've lured the dead in. That's what we're chasing."

Munroe narrowed his eyes slightly, catching the careful wording. "Runaways?" he repeated, skeptical.

"Yeah," Bellamy said, locking eyes with him. "That's how the zombies got in. Ellis wants them found."

Munroe held his gaze for a beat longer than the others, then nodded slowly. "Okay, boss." They didn't press. Bellamy didn't expect them to. His team knew when to follow orders and when to ask questions and this wasn't one of those times.

Within twenty minutes, the van was loaded. Ammo, restraints, maps, and food. Bellamy took the wheel. As they pulled out of Kinross, the gates closed behind them with a heavy, metallic groan. No one spoke for a while. Bellamy's mind churned as the road stretched out in front of them. People. He wants people. Fresh test subjects. He had no idea what he was going to do when they actually found someone. But one thing was certain. Ellis had to be stopped.

Bellamy's team had been out for a few hours now, slowly making their way through the empty roads and lifeless streets. The van crawled by abandoned houses, overgrown storefronts, and rusted-out vehicles. Occasionally, they'd stop, step out with weapons drawn, and check interiors for any sign of the supposed "runaways."

But so far, nothing. "This is a waste of time," Raven finally said, resting her boots on the dashboard, frustration dripping from his voice. "They could be anywhere, if they even exist."

Bellamy pulled the van to the side of the road and killed the engine. "Right," he said, turning in his seat to face them. "I need to tell you something." The sudden seriousness in his tone wiped the weariness from their expressions. Ortega leaned forward. Munroe, sitting beside Raven, shifted uncomfortably. "I lied," Bellamy began. "Those runaways? They don't exist. The breach... it wasn't from outside." He went on, telling them everything, about Ellis's secret lab beneath Kinross, the grotesque experiments, the new serum he called ZF-16s. About how the power surge set off an alarm that triggered the infected. About Dr. Mirak's team being slaughtered. He told them of the note he received and the midnight meeting under the railway bridge.

And then he told them the rest.

"There are more labs. Four more. The biggest ones in a town called Rose Bank, inside an old tech building with a warehouse out back. There's over a hundred infected in there, Ellis is trying to perfect control over them." Silence. The van was still, the only sound the wind howling through broken windows of nearby buildings.

Ortega finally spoke, voice cold. "Count me out. I'm not dragging innocent people back so Ellis can cut them open and see what makes them tick."

The others nodded. Raven cursed under her breath. Munroe just stared at Bellamy, betrayed but more angry than shocked. Bellamy raised his hands.

"That's not the plan. We're not handing anyone over to Ellis. If we find survivors, we help them. But I want eyes on that Rose Bank facility. If it's real… we destroy it."

Raven leaned back, arms crossed. "And how do you plan on doing that?"

Bellamy gave a grim smile. "Good thing I brought C4," Ortega added, pulling a small duffel out from under his seat. The team shared a look, this wasn't just another run. This was a war. A line had been crossed. Bellamy started the van. They turned north, heading for Rose Bank.

The sun was starting to fall as they left the broken highway behind. In the distance, the silhouette of the old tech complex came into view, a tall building surrounded by chain-link fences and patrolled by figures they couldn't quite make out yet. But as they rolled to a stop a few hundred meters out, Bellamy lifted his binoculars. His stomach dropped. "They're guarding it," he muttered.

Raven glanced over. "Who?"

Bellamy lowered the binoculars. "People, armed. Must be Ellis's men, but I don't recognize any of them. That's not good." They stayed hidden in the tree line, watching the compound. Vehicles parked outside. Movement in and out of the warehouse. Bellamy noted everything. This wasn't going to be a hit-and-run. This was going to take planning. Timing. And maybe, sacrifice.

But one thing was now certain. Rose Bank was real.

Chapter 25 – Rose Bank and Further

Bellamy lay prone on the ridge overlooking the old tech facility in Rose Bank. Through his binoculars, he had spent hours observing the pattern of the guards, noting every shift change, every patrol route, and every moment of carelessness. The building stood cold and imposing beneath the grey afternoon sky, its walls stained with age and menace.

He'd counted ten guards, all armed and alert, stationed around the perimeter and inside the compound. There were at least six scientists, most of them wearing stained white coats and moving back and forth between the main building and the warehouse. Every so often, a side door would open, and two guards would drag out a corpse, another zombie that hadn't responded to their conditioning. Some were riddled with bullets. Others had strange scars, surgical openings that made Bellamy sick to look at. Failed experiments. He slid back down the ridge and jogged the half-mile back to where the others were holed up in a derelict farmhouse. "They're definitely doing what the scientists warned us about," he said as he approached. The team looked up, gathered around a small fire they'd managed to light with scrap wood and some dry insulation from the attic.

"What'd you see?" Ortega asked, tossing a half-eaten protein bar into his bag.

"Ten guards. Six scientists. They're testing the infected, trying to control them, just like Ellis. Every once in a while, they bring a body out, must be the ones that couldn't be controlled or reacted violently. They just dump them behind the warehouse like trash."

"Disgusting," Raven muttered. "Any sign of survivors? Prisoners?"

Bellamy shook his head. "Not from what I could see. Either they haven't brought in new test subjects recently, or they're keeping them locked deep inside."

Munroe leaned forward, his face grim. "So what's the plan? We can't just sit here."

Bellamy nodded. "We won't. We wait until nightfall. I want to get closer and see if there's a way in that's not guarded. Ortega, bring the C4. We might not be able to get everyone out or destroy the whole place, but we can do some serious damage."

"You thinking we plant it on the lab building?" Raven asked.

"Exactly," Bellamy replied. "Take out their equipment, their data. Set them back months. Maybe more." The team nodded in agreement, the firelight flickering over their determined expressions.

Ortega pulled the C4 kit from his bag and started checking the wiring. "They wanna play God? Let's blow their temple sky high."

As the sun dipped below the horizon, and the cold crept in around them, Bellamy stood silently looking toward Rose Bank. This place, this lab, it was just one head of the monster Ellis was building. But tonight, they'd start cutting it down. The moon was high, casting a silver hue over the cracked tarmac and rusting fences surrounding the Rose Bank facility. Bellamy moved silently through the brush, Raven just behind him, crouching low as they reached the rear perimeter.

"Are Raven and Munroe in position?" Bellamy whispered. Ortega nodded. Back near the south fence. I've got the C4. Bellamy adjusted his grip on the suppressed rifle. "Good. We'll check the vents here to see if we can find a way in and plant the charges near the labs. Worst-case, we signal them to start the detonation and pull out." He crept closer to the fence. A single guard was stationed near the warehouse's loading dock, idly smoking and leaning against the wall. Bellamy signaled to Ortega, who pulled out a throwing knife, took careful aim, and sent it flying. The guard slumped to the ground without a sound. They scaled the fence, avoiding the floodlights that periodically scanned the area, and made their way to the rear wall of the main building. There, just as Bellamy had seen earlier, was a vent large enough for someone to crawl through. Ortega unscrewed the grating, and the two of them slipped inside, the metal cool and silent beneath them. The air smelled of chemicals and decay. A few minutes of crawling brought them to a grate overlooking the central lab.

Bellamy's breath caught.

Below them, a glass-walled room held three zombies chained to the floor by steel collars. Electrodes were attached to their heads. Scientists moved around them with tablet devices, monitoring vitals. One of the undead was barely recognizable, its skin pale and veined, eyes glazed, but unlike the others, it didn't thrash or snarl. "They're responding to commands," one scientist said. "ZF-17 batch is more stable." "For now," another replied. "You saw what happened in Kinross. One surge and they tear through everything." Bellamy turned to Ortega, jaw clenched. He mouthed one word: Enough. They backed out of the vent and slipped down the side of the building. At the south fence, Munroe and Raven waited.

"Plant it near the lab wall," Bellamy ordered. "Give us five minutes to clear, then blow it." Ortega didn't say a word. He handed out small earpieces for comms and got to work, pressing the charges into place and setting the timer. The digital countdown blinked silently.

4:59... 4:58...

The team moved fast, cutting back through the fence and into the treeline. Just as they hit the ridge, Bellamy turned for one last look.

BOOM!

The blast was massive, far bigger than what any of them expected. A shockwave rippled through the treeline, knocking loose branches and sending a flock of birds screeching into the night sky.

"What the hell was that?" Munroe yelled, ducking instinctively behind a log.

Raven, eyes wide, turned toward Bellamy. "That… was bigger than C4. There must've been something else on the other side of that wall. Maybe fuel or… some kind of chemical storage?"

Bellamy stared at the plume of black smoke rising high into the sky, fire licking through what remained of the warehouse roof. "If they were storing anything volatile, accelerants, test samples, even more of those things we just blew it all sky-high."

"Shit," Ortega said, shielding his eyes as the heat rolled in waves. "Well that lab is fucked, nothing is getting out of there."

Bellamy's jaw tightened. "We've just hit a nerve. Ellis will feel this. We need to move, now."

"Where to?" Raven asked, already checking her weapon.

Bellamy reached into his pack and pulled out the map Harold had given him. He circled two locations with his finger: the biscuit factory near Tannochside, and the Braveheart Gym near Burnside. "We split up. I'll take Raven to Braveheart. Munroe, Ortega, you check out the biscuit factory. In and out. Recon only. We will regroup in 48 hours."

Ortega gave a low whistle. "You sure splitting up's a good idea?"

Bellamy's eyes were still on the flames. "Ellis will be moving pieces as soon as he finds out what's happened. If we want to stop what he's building, we need to move faster than he can react."

Raven gave him a curt nod. "Let's burn it all down, then."

The team gave quick nods and one last look at the inferno now lighting up the Rose Bank skyline. Then they vanished into the shadows, each heading toward their next mission, carrying with them the weight of what they'd seen... and what they'd just destroyed.

Bellamy and Raven crouched low on the hillside overlooking the Braveheart Gym, a once-bustling community fitness centre now twisted into something far more sinister. The building was modest in size, not nearly as large as Rose Bank, but it still had five armed guards patrolling the perimeter and at least six white-coated scientists moving in and out through a rear entrance.

"Same setup," Bellamy muttered, scanning the scene through a pair of old binoculars. "Guards, lab coats, and the occasional zombie being dragged out back and shot when it doesn't obey."

"Same shit, different place," Raven whispered. They observed for hours, documenting routines and noting weaknesses. The guards weren't especially alert, likely not expecting anyone brave or stupid enough to strike.

Then Raven's sharp eyes caught something. "Bellamy," she said, nudging him with her elbow, "look over there, about 200 yards out. Diesel tanker."

Bellamy followed her gaze. The battered tanker sat idle near a rusted-out garage, half-covered in vines. "If that thing still has fuel..."

"We could drive it straight through the gym," Raven finished for him, a grin spreading across his face. "Blow the whole place sky-high like we did at Rose Bank."

Bellamy gave a slow, approving nod. "Let's check it out." They crept down the slope and approached the tanker cautiously. A quick check revealed it was indeed half full, and miraculously, the keys were still in the ignition. Bellamy climbed into the cab, gave the key a turn and the engine coughed to life. "Beautiful," he muttered, guiding the truck in a wide arc to the top of the hill overlooking the gym. Once in position, he jammed a rod through the wheel to keep it straight and glanced at Raven.

"Time to light another match. Put some c4 on the tanker near the fuel tank." He released the brake, and the truck started to roll. The tanker picked up speed as it barreled downhill. By the time it hit the gym, it was a screaming juggernaut of steel and fuel. The guards shouted in panic, diving out of the way as the truck smashed through the gym's front entrance like a battering ram.

BOOM!

The explosion was thunderous. Fire engulfed the building, the shockwave sending debris into the air and flattening everything in the immediate area. Screams rang out, human and otherwise as the roaring flames consumed the gym and everything inside. Then came the groaning. From beneath the wreckage, the unmistakable sound of the undead rose. The heat and destruction had awakened something, or someone.

"NOW, RAVEN!" Bellamy roared.

Raven didn't hesitate. She clicked the detonator.

BOOM!

A second explosion erupted, turning the already-flaming gym into a smouldering crater of fire and twisted metal. A wave of intense heat hit them as they ducked down behind cover. When the dust settled, one of the guards lay writhing on the ground, his leg engulfed in flames, screaming in agony. Bellamy rushed forward, stomping out the fire with a torn blanket he grabbed from the van. The man passed out from the pain.

Raven looked at Bellamy, eyebrows raised. "What now?" Bellamy didn't answer at first. He knelt, pulled a zip-tie from his pocket, and secured the unconscious guard's wrists. Then he hoisted the man over his shoulder and dumped him into the back of the van.

"If Ellis wants test subjects," Bellamy said coldly, "he can have his own men." He slammed the doors shut.

Ortega and Munroe pulled the van over half a mile from the target, an old biscuit factory on the outskirts of Tannochside. From the outside, it looked unassuming, another relic of the pre-apocalypse industry. But the intel said otherwise. The two of them slipped out quietly, moving fast but low through the crumbling streets until they reached the edge of a three-story office block nearby. Inside, they found stairs mostly intact and made their way up to the roof. Once they got to the top, both men dropped to their bellies and pulled out binoculars.

The view confirmed their unease. The factory was surrounded by a wire mesh fence, thick with old barbed reinforcement. But that wasn't the troubling part. The yard was full of zombies. At least two dozen, some still wearing what were clearly lab coats, others in ragged military gear, rifles still strapped to their decaying backs. They shuffled aimlessly, groaning softly, trapped but still dangerous. Munroe exhaled through his nose, lowering his binoculars.

"The same thing that happened at Kinross must have happened here." "Another failed test," Ortega muttered. "They lost control, and the dead overran the place." The two sat in silence for a long moment, watching the dead stagger around the yard. "What do we do?" Ortega asked. "Just leave?"

Munroe thought for a second, then gave a firm nod. "This place is done. Whatever Ellis had going on here is already dead.. or undead. We meet Bellamy outside the last lab, Kintyre, as agreed."

Ortega looked one more time through his binoculars before standing. "Let's hope Kintyre isn't worse." Without another word they descended from the roof, slipped back to the van, and disappeared into the growing dusk headed south to what was once the Kintyre settlement.

As Bellamy and Raven prepped their gear, ready to head south toward the final lab site at Kintyre, movement on the horizon caught Bellamy's eye. He squinted, look, there, tearing away from a nearby village, was a van. Moving fast.

Raven raised her head. "You see that?"

"Yeah," Bellamy muttered. "Van. Heading out in a hurry."

"More of Ellis's men?"

"I don't know. Might be someone that's seen what happened and is enroute to tell Ellis." Bellamy watched the dust trail rising behind it, thoughtful. "We should tail it. See where they're going."

Raven gave a slow nod. "Could be nothing. Could be something. Either way if it is one of Ellis's people, we can't let them tell him. Not yet," Raven says.

They jumped into their van and followed, keeping a careful distance. The van ahead never stopped, powering through open roads, twisting through the remains of the countryside. Bellamy kept the lights off, sticking to the tree lines when he could. After a few hours, Raven sat up straighter. "You seeing this?"

On the horizon, rising like a monolith through the early morning haze, was a prison, intact, reinforced, and clearly occupied. Watchtowers. Fencing. A settlement. Bellamy narrowed his eyes. "That's not one of Ellis's. I was never told about this place."

"You sure?"

Bellamy shook his head. "Not on any map. Not in any report. This isn't his." They pulled the van up about a mile out and ditched it in the woods. Stealth was the best move now. They moved low and quick through the trees, stopping just at the edge of the clearing. The prison's massive front gates were slowly closing, whoever had arrived in that van had just gone in.

Bellamy squinted and then froze. He recognized someone. Raven noticed. "What?" Bellamy took a deep breath.

"Drop your weapons in the van."

"What?! Are you nuts?" Raven hissed. "You said this could be hostile!"

"Maybe," Bellamy said calmly, eyes still fixed on the gate. "But if I'm right, we just found an edge. Might've found help." He looked at Raven with a small, wry grin. "The enemy of my enemy... right?" Raven grumbled but nodded, pulling her sidearm free and stashing it back in the van.

They waited through the night, concealed in the trees, watching the place come to life as dawn lit the horizon. As the morning sun rose, they stepped out of the treeline, hands raised, walking up the open path to the front gates.

A voice shouted. "People are approaching!" Guards shifted into position. A moment later, Callum stood on the wall, rifle in hand. He leaned over the edge and squinted. Alarm raised. Moments later, Derek ran up, still adjusting the strap on his weapon. He climbed the ladder to the tower, looked down and his face dropped. His voice echoed across the yard.

"Oh no... you again."

"Bellamy!" Derek shouted from behind the wall. "Give me one good reason I don't put a bolt through your brain right now and be done with you!"

Bellamy raised his hands slowly, his voice calm. "Derek, I'm unarmed. So is Raven. No weapons. They're in the van at the tree line to the east."

Callum quickly slung his rifle and scanned through his scope. "I see it. Van checks out.. but that's all." By now, Derek stood at the gate, five others behind him, rifles, bows, crossbows raised, tense and ready to fire.

"Keep 'em still or I'll shoot," Derek growled, Daryl, Bill, search them."

The two men moved fast, thorough. Bellamy and Raven didn't resist.

"Clean," Daryl confirmed, stepping back.

"Same here," Bill added.

At the same time, Maggie arrived at the van. Her voice came through the radio, tense. "Weapons in the front... back's locked." She opened it. "Uh... we've got someone here. Tied up. Unconscious but alive."

Derek's eyes narrowed. "Explain."

"Let us in and I'll explain everything," Bellamy said.

Derek hesitated, fury in his eyes. "You think I'm letting you stroll in here after everything you've done?"

"You can blindfold us," Bellamy replied. "Cable tie us. Whatever you want. But you need to hear this, Derek. It's bigger than you think."

Derek glared, jaw clenched, but after a long pause, he nodded once. "Blindfold them. Zip-tie their hands. And don't speak unless spoken to."

Raven whispered under her breath, "This better be worth it." Bellamy didn't respond. They were blindfolded, tied, and marched through the gates. The sounds of the prison community echoed around them, people, movement, a place alive.

After a few minutes of walking, they were sat in chairs, the zip-ties still tight around their wrists. The blindfolds came off. Derek stood in front of them, arms folded, the full council gathered behind him, Jennifer, Callum, Anne, Daryl, Maggie, even young Sam watching from a corner.

"Alright," Derek said coldly. "Five minutes. Then you're zombie bait. Start talking."

Bellamy took a breath. "I'll make it count." He didn't hold back. He told them everything starting with Ellis and Kinross. The secret labs. The failed experiments. The controlled zombies. The breakout that killed dozens. Then Rose Bank. Brave Heart. The maps and notes he'd been given. The captured scientist he brought as proof.

Daryl, arms crossed, interrupted. "Why should we trust this piece of filth? He tried to kill us."

"I was acting for my people," Bellamy shot back. "At the time, I didn't know who you were. I followed Ellis because he promised safety. Structure. But I've seen what he's really doing. I lost friends in that lab, good people. He doesn't care who dies for his cause. I've had enough." He nodded at the notes Daryl had pulled from his pocket. "Everything you need to confirm my story is there. Maps. Coordinates. Even some of the science Ellis is using. He's not trying to survive, he's trying to rule. And anyone who doesn't fall in line... he'll send the dead after them."

The room fell quiet. The council exchanged glances. Suspicion. Fear. But something else, too, curiosity.

Truth.

Bellamy leaned forward as far as the zip-ties would allow. "I'm not here to fight. I'm here because I think we want the same thing, Ellis gone. This war's coming whether you like it or not. But I'd rather fight it with you than against you." He looked straight at Derek. "The enemy of my enemy... right?"

Derek stared at Bellamy, his face unreadable. Without a word, he turned away. "Blindfold them. Throw them in the hole." Two guards moved forward, tightening the cable ties and pulling blindfolds back over Bellamy and Raven's heads. "Two guards on them at all times," Derek added, glancing at Stephen and Ross. "That's you two. Don't sleep. Don't blink." Stephen and Ross exchanged a quick nod, then hauled Bellamy and Raven away. They were thrown into the old segregation block "the hole" as it used to be known. Cold concrete, rusted bars, no windows. Just a single flickering bulb and silence.

Outside, in the main hall of the prison, the council gathered again. "We should throw them to the zombies," Maggie said flatly, leaning on the table. "Right into the trench. No trial, no risk. Let them scream like the ones they've helped Ellis kill."

"I second that," Daryl added. "Same guy who tried to kill Derek, Jennifer and me not that long ago. I don't buy this sudden change of heart."

Lee nodded. "Sounds like he's just saying what we want to hear."

Jennifer, arms crossed, leaned forward. "But what if he's not lying? What if Ellis really is building an army? We can't ignore the possibility. Look at those things he sent after us at the school. If he has more of them that he can control then we might not have a chance of survival." She says

Jillian agreed. "If there's even a chance it's true, it means we're already in danger. That psycho could be on his way here right now."

The room locked in a heated debate.

Then Derek raised his hand, voice cutting through the debate. "Enough." He looked around the table. "Okay. So we have a decision to make, do we trust them, or not?"

Callum cleared his throat. "We don't need to trust them yet. We check out what they said. Recon only. No contact. No heroics. If it looks bad, we fall back." He laid a map on the table, pointing at the locations Bellamy had given them. "Rose Bank. Brave Heart. Tannochside. Each one's barely an hour from here. We send out three teams. Quiet, fast, in and out."

Maggie sighed. "Fine. But we go armed. "The council nodded in agreement.

"Three teams of two," Derek said, scanning the room. "We keep the prison fully guarded."

"Daryl and Bill, you're Team One. You two check out Brave Heart."

"Got it," Daryl said.

"Callum and Lee, you're Team Two. Check out Tannochside."

"On it," Callum nodded.

Derek looked to Maggie about to name her for the final team, when Jillian stepped forward. "I'll go with you," she said.

Daryl blinked. "You sure?"

"I've been training with Maggie and you, Daryl. I'm ready for this," Jillian said firmly.

Jennifer nodded. "She's more than ready."

Derek gave her a long look, then finally nodded. "Alright. Jillian and I will check out Rose Bank."

The council quickly approved the plan. Vehicles were readied, bags packed. Each team was issued radios, maps, weapons, and orders to observe only.

Bellamy and Raven sat in the dark cell, unaware of the decision made above them. But the clock had started ticking.

Derek stood in the car park just outside New Haven's garage. The three teams were gathered in front of him, gear packed, engines idling. The dawn light spilled across the cracked tarmac, casting long shadows as Derek's voice turned low and serious. "Alright, listen up. Only myself, Jennifer, and Maggie know this, but now you do too." He gestured toward the south. "About half a mile south of here, there's an old bakery. Looks abandoned. Out back, there's a metal shelving unit against the far wall. Behind it is a tunnel." Everyone leaned in, listening carefully. "You climb down the first ladder into the tunnel system. Now this bit's important, so listen close. Once you're down, go straight until you hit three ladders. Turn right. Go past two more ladders, then left, and straight to the end. There's a metal door. Code is 1819."

He looked each of them in the eye. "It'll bring you out in the lobby behind the front desk, inside New Haven's walls. Only a few of us know about it. Cameras are up, and we've got shifts watching the monitors. If things go south and you're being chased or need a way back in, use the tunnel. Now that we've got power back, we can lock the place from the inside. Use it to trap anyone... or anything." He paused. "Repeat it back."

Callum went first. Followed by the rest. "Three ladders. Turn right. Pass two more. Turn left. Straight to the end. Code 1819."

"Good," Derek nodded. "That's your lifeline. Don't forget it." Jillian, Daryl, Lee, Bill, and Callum all nodded in unison. Derek exhaled. "Alright. Let's move out."

Daryl and Bill headed to Brave Hearts Gym. The old gym still reeked of scorched metal and death. Daryl steered the truck off the road, parking behind the remains of a burned-out van. They approached cautiously, rifles drawn. The blast site was still smoldering in places, but the gym was completely destroyed, twisted metal, concrete shards, and soot-blackened bodies scattered across the lot.

"No one's making it outta that," [8]Bill muttered.

Daryl scanned the wreckage. "Look at this." They approached a half-buried body with a lab coat on, a charred badge melted to the chest. "Scientist," Daryl confirmed. "

Bellamy wasn't lying," Bill said. "The place was crawling with these freaks."

They took photos, pocketed a few scorched documents, and backed out. Daryl gave one last look at the rubble before getting in the truck.

Callum and Lee headed to Tannochside. The perimeter fence still buzzed with tension. Callum lay on his belly, binoculars up, Lee beside him. Inside the wire, the yard was crawling with zombies. Some still wore lab gear. Others clutched rifles, their arms stiff in death, some missing limbs.

"This place went to hell too," Lee whispered.

"Same story," Callum said. "Something broke containment." They spotted what looked like a breach in the fencing, twisted wire, a smeared trail of blood leading away from the factory. "We don't go in," Callum reminded him. "Recon only." They took photos, and quietly crept back to the truck.

Derek slowed the vehicle to a stop as the burnt, skeletal remains of the Rose Bank warehouse came into view. Jillian leaned forward in her seat, eyes scanning the blackened wreckage through the cracked windshield.

"Jesus..." she muttered. "It's exactly like Bellamy said."

Derek said nothing as he stepped out, boots crunching over charred gravel and twisted debris. The air still held a faint trace of smoke and scorched chemicals. He pulled his scarf tighter over his mouth as Jillian followed behind, her eyes wide as they walked into the remnants of the lab. The destruction was absolute. Walls were blown inward, steel beams curled from the heat of the blast. A massive hole gaped where one side of the building used to be. Burnt-out lab equipment littered the area, fragments of shattered glass, blackened control panels, and the occasional twisted, half-melted chair or desk. They passed what used to be the loading bay. Jillian paused, crouching near a pile of scorched bodies, barely recognizable. Some wore the remains of lab coats. Others had military gear fused to their corpses.

"Charred... but you can still see the zips on their suits," she whispered. "Some of them were infected."

Derek walked ahead, eyeing the collapsed interior. Torn-open containment units. Scorch marks trailing across the floor like something exploded from the inside. Bellamy hadn't been lying. He exhaled slowly, jaw tightening. "He told the truth."

Jillian looked over at him. "You believe him now?"

"I believe what he said about Rose Bank," Derek replied, scanning the ruins. "Doesn't mean I trust him. But this... this lines up."

Jillian stood beside him, silent for a moment as the wind blew ash through the skeletal remains of the warehouse. "How many more of these do you think Ellis has?"

Derek shook his head. "Too many."

They lingered a moment longer before Jillian pulled out her camera, snapping photos of the destruction, the charred dead, the broken remnants of whatever twisted research had gone on here.

"We'll show the council," Derek said. "Let them see it for themselves."

"And if they still don't trust him?" Jillian asked.

Derek glanced around at the wreckage again. "Then they need to ask themselves one question…" he said quietly. "If this was one of his labs… how long until the next one is aimed at us?

The engine hummed softly as the van made its way back toward New Haven. Jillian had one hand on the wheel, the other resting lazily on the gear stick. Derek sat in the passenger seat, eyes distant, locked on the road ahead but not really seeing it.He wasn't thinking about the destroyed warehouse. Not even Ellis. His mind had wandered elsewhere, to that night. The one he had convinced himself was a dream. Or was it?

Jillian glanced sideways at him, catching the furrow in his brow. "You look deep in thought," she said, her voice gentle but curious. "What's up?"

Derek stirred from his haze, cleared his throat. "Just thinking… if we can trust Bellamy or not." It wasn't a lie. Not exactly.

Jillian nodded, her fingers tapping lightly on the wheel. "We'll decide together," she said, keeping her eyes on the road. "Don't worry, okay?"

Derek gave a quiet nod and looked away again. But he could feel her gaze flicking to him when she thought he wasn't looking. Each time she glanced over, there was a small smile tugging at the corner of her mouth. Subtle, almost hesitant. Was it kindness? Was it something else? Was it real? He leaned his elbow on the window and looked out at the trees streaking past. The memory was vivid, too vivid to be a dream. Her hand in his. That closeness. The whisper of something more in the middle of all this madness. But she'd never brought it up. And maybe that meant it hadn't happened at all.

Or maybe she was waiting for him to say something.. Derek closed his eyes for a moment. He wasn't sure what was more terrifying, the dead outside the walls... or the truth he might have to face inside them. Only time would tell.

All three teams had returned now. The council gathered in the meeting room, the atmosphere thick with tension and silent anticipation. Photos were spread across the table, charred rubble, scorched bodies, bloodied white coats. Everything Bellamy had claimed... was true.

"He told the truth," Callum said firmly, setting one of the photos down. No one argued.

Derek stepped away and keyed his radio. "Steph, bring them in." Minutes later, Bellamy and Raven were escorted into the room. They were seated across from the council, eyes alert but calm.

Derek folded his arms. "Alright, Bellamy. Your story checks out so far. What's your next move?"

Bellamy nodded. "I'm meeting Ortega and Munroe at Kintyre. That's the last known lab. But it's the most dangerous. The zombies got out there, wiped out the whole settlement. Over 300 people dead. There were over 100 in the lab alone."

The room went still.

"I'll leave after that. No one will hear a word about New Haven," Bellamy continued. He turned to Raven. "And if I talk, if I betray any of you she'll kill me."

Raven nodded without hesitation. "Swear on my kids' lives. I'll stab or shoot him without blinking." The blunt honesty silenced the room.

Callum leaned forward. "Okay, so what do you want from us?"

Bellamy gestured slightly. "You saw the guy in the van. We're meant to be gathering fresh test subjects for Ellis, people not yet turned. That's his new plan. But instead of helping him, we're going to trap him. We lock his guards in the old police cells, make it look like a success, lure him in and take him out." He looked around the room. "Ellis has maybe ten to twelve loyal bodyguards. The rest? They follow me."

Derek exchanged a look with Callum. "You want us to come to Kintyre with you?"

"Yes," Bellamy replied. "There's four of us. We need four of yours. You help us round up the rest of Ellis's men, lock them down, then we draw him out and finish this."

Derek nodded slowly, then turned. "Callum. Daryl. Bill. You're with me."

The group moved quickly. The van was loaded, weapons checked. True to their word, Bellamy and Raven sat in the back, hands loosely bound for appearances.

As they prepped, Raven leaned toward Bellamy. "Why are you agreeing to be tied up? To play the prisoner?"

"If this is what it takes for them to trust us," Bellamy said, "then so be it. I'm tired, Raven. Tired of fighting everyone. There's more of the dead than the living now. We should be working together, not tearing each other apart."

Raven gave a quiet nod, understanding in her eyes.

Just before departure, Jennifer walked up to Derek. Without a word, she cupped his face and kissed him, firm and full of emotion. Then she leaned close and whispered, "Be careful out there. Any sign of trouble, bolt them. Come back to me."

Derek smiled. "Of course I will, Jen. I'll see you soon."

The gate creaked open. Engines rumbled to life. Old enemies now allies, they drove out toward Kintyre, towards the final battleground that would decide not just their fates, but possibly the future of what was left of the world.

As the gates of New Haven clanked shut and the convoy disappeared into the distance, Jillian remained still. Her heart thudded in her chest, not from fear but from guilt. What she had done, what she had hidden, had happened just two nights ago. And she couldn't carry the weight of it any longer. She turned and walked purposefully toward the chapel.

Inside, soft candlelight flickered against the old stone walls. Jennifer and Anne were already there, kneeling at the altar, heads bowed in quiet prayer for their loved ones. Jillian knelt beside them silently, her hands clasped, trying to summon the courage she needed. After a while, the others stood and left, giving her a gentle squeeze of the shoulder as they passed. Jillian stayed.

Moments later, Father Luke stepped in, closing the door behind him. His eyes found hers. "Jillian," he said with quiet warmth. "Would you like to talk?"

"I... I need to confess," she said. "Please."

He gave a solemn nod and walked to the confessional booth. Jillian followed, stepping inside and sitting down. The small wooden screen separated them, but it didn't hide the anxiety in her voice.

"In the name of the Father, and of the Son, and of the Holy Spirit," Father Luke began. "Speak freely, my child."

Jillian took a deep breath, her fingers trembling. "Forgive me, Father, for I have sinned."

"How have you sinned, my child?"

Her voice cracked as she spoke.

"It was two nights ago. Here. In New Haven... Derek and I... we slept together." She paused as the words hung in the air. "It wasn't just a moment of weakness. It meant something. We stayed up talking, connected like we haven't in years. We made love. We held each other all night." She swallowed hard. "But before dawn, he fell asleep. And I panicked. I got dressed. I left. And when he found me the next morning and asked what had happened... I lied. I told him that I didn't turn up, I let him think he had dreamt it." Tears welled in her eyes. "I couldn't face the truth. Not with Jennifer here. Not with everything going on. I thought I was protecting them, him, her, even myself. But now I don't know. I don't know anything anymore."

There was silence for a long moment. Then Father Luke's voice came, calm and gentle. "You carry a heavy burden, Jillian. You acted from fear, and that fear led you to lie. But what you're doing now by speaking the truth, is the first step to redemption."

"I feel like a coward," she whispered.

"You're human," Father Luke said. "You made a choice in the moment, but now you face another one. You can continue the lie... or you can face the truth and whatever comes with it."

She sat in silence, breathing deeply. "I don't know if he'll forgive me. I don't even know if I want him to."

"Then start by forgiving yourself," Father Luke said. "And when the time comes, speak honestly. No matter how hard it is."

Jillian nodded slowly, her guilt laid bare in the flickering light of the chapel. She had taken the first step. But there were more to come.

The van rumbled over the cracked road and came to a halt just outside the old farm access point near Kintyre. Ortega and Munroe were already there, standing casually by their vehicle with rifles slung and a firepit smoking gently nearby. As the van doors opened,

Ortega chuckled and shouted, "You took your bloody time!" But his grin vanished as Derek, Daryl, Bill, and Callum poured out of the van with weapons raised, their movements sharp and deliberate.

"Drop your weapons! Now!" Callum barked.

Ortega and Munroe froze, stunned. Then Bellamy stepped out of the van, still partially bound, supported by Callum. "Stand down," he ordered sharply to his men. "Do as they say. It's fine." With narrowed eyes and a slow nod, Ortega and Munroe dropped their weapons.

Derek approached with firm authority. "Untie them," he said to Callum, nodding toward Bellamy and Raven. As the last of the cable ties fell away, Bellamy flexed his wrists and looked Derek square in the eyes.

"It's dangerous to go in there without weapons," he said plainly. "I give you my word, Derek, none of my people will lay a finger on yours. We all want the same thing now."

Derek considered him for a moment, his gaze unwavering. Then he stepped forward and pressed a pistol and a knife into Bellamy's hands. Bellamy blinked, surprised. But before he could speak, Derek leaned in closer and pointed up toward the ridge of the hill behind them. "See that rooftop?" Bellamy followed his gaze and saw a faint shimmer of scopes catching the early morning light. "I've got four snipers up there," Derek said, voice low and firm. "Each one could shoot the seed out of an apple at 500 yards. Try anything... and you and your men will be zombie feed." Bellamy looked back at Derek, this time with something new in his eyes, respect.

"I swear, Derek. Nothing will happen on my watch. Not now. Not anymore."

Derek gave a curt nod. "Good."

With the tension slightly eased, the group gathered their gear, checking weapons and distributing what little ammunition they had between them. The ridge snipers gave subtle signals, clear, for now. Together, the unlikely allies began to move toward the Kintyre lab, the final known site of Ellis's dark experiments. Whatever waited inside, they would face it together, each step forward a test of trust, truth, and survival.

Chapter 26 – The Last Lab

The sun dipped low behind a blanket of grey clouds as the group reached the observation point, a derelict building some 200 yards from their target. One by one, they scaled the old staircase to the roof, crouching low against the parapet as they took in the sight before them.

The lab sat within towering, seven-foot-high reinforced walls. Outside, a thick sea of the dead pressed and clawed at the barricade, hundreds, maybe thousands, all moaning and shifting in endless hunger. Inside the perimeter, they counted five guards stationed at key points, and another five inside the main structure, visible only through fleeting shadows and movements. Scientists in white coats moved nervously in and out of side buildings, unaware they were being watched.

"It's like a fortress," Daryl muttered. "No gates, no ladders.. How the hell do they get in or out?"

"Maybe they don't," Bill says. "Maybe Ellis left them there. Sealed in."

Derek's eyes narrowed. "That place is crawling with zombies on the outside and guards on the inside. That's a death trap to storm head-on."

Bellamy turned to Munroe. "Any C4 left?"

Munroe nodded. "Two bricks. But only one detonator. We found some old dynamite too, enough for a couple of distractions."

Bellamy smirked. "Perfect. Here's the plan, if everyone's on board."

They all leaned in. "We throw dynamite far from the walls. Lure the horde away. Then Daryl will fire a bolt with the c4 attached to the outer wall, I'll hit the C4 with my rifle, blasting a hole in the inner compound. Raven ties the last stick of dynamite to a crossbow bolt and Derek hits the lab's doors at the same time. When the zombies rush back in, the guards won't stand a chance."

Derek folded his arms. "And the prisoners you promised Ellis?"

"I'll lie," Bellamy said simply. "Get him to come down without his security. That's all I need."

No one objected. They all knew what had to be done. Callum and Ortega lit their fuses and hurled the dynamite sticks over the rooftops. Twin explosions rocked the nearby fields. As expected, the horde shifted, groaning and stumbling toward the sound. Every single guard ran from the building to the walls, yelling, trying to bring the horde back to the walls. Now. Raven tied the final stick of dynamite to Daryl's bolt and lit it.

"Now!" Bellamy barked.

Daryl fired, the bolt screaming through the air and striking the heavy lab doors with a metallic clang.

Simultaneously, Derek squeezed the trigger on his rifle, hitting the charge on the far wall. A thunderous blast tore through the concrete. A moment of silence.

Then the dam broke.

The horde surged back, pouring into the compound like a flood of death. Screams erupted, guards and scientists alike overwhelmed in seconds. Through it all, the group watched from the rooftop, silent, still.

Ten minutes passed. Then the screaming stopped. They thought it was over, until the lab exploded. The fireball ripped through the air with a deafening roar, the shockwave hurling the group backward off the rooftop. They hit the streets below in a tangled mess.

Groans followed. Most landed on crates, bushes, or dirt. But Raven hadn't been so lucky. She was impaled on the jagged spikes of an old perimeter fence, blood already soaking her leg. Callum screamed, his leg bent awkwardly beneath him.

"Shit!" Derek yelled. "The horde's coming back!"

They could hear the groaning already, closer now, drawn by the screaming of Raven and Callum.

"Grab Callum!" Daryl shouted, limping to help. Bellamy moved to help too.

Bill tugged Derek's arm. "We have to move! Now!"

They tried to lift Raven but she shook her head, teeth clenched through the pain. "If you pull me off this, I'll bleed out in seconds. Just go."

"We're not leaving you—" Derek started to say.

"Go!" she shouted. Then softly, "Please." As they backed away, Raven looked them all in the eyes, then raised her pistol. Bang. She collapsed forward, lifeless. The horde arrived seconds later, a rolling wave of death.

"Move!" Bill screamed.

The group scrambled, dragging Callum with them. They threw open the van doors and piled in, Daryl hitting the gas the moment the last door slammed shut. As the van tore away from Kintyre, smoke billowed behind them. The lab was gone. Ellis's last stronghold, destroyed. But the cost... had been steep.

No one spoke as the van roared down the road. The silence was heavier than the explosion itself. They had done it. But they were bleeding. Inside and out. The van skidded to a halt near the ridge where the sniper team waited, weapons trained on the vehicle. Bellamy and his group began to step out cautiously. The snipers' fingers twitched on triggers, eyes sharp as hawks.

"What the hell is this?" Bellamy barked, his voice cutting through the tension like a knife. "I thought you trusted me."

Derek emerged from the van, hands raised slightly in a calming gesture. "Guns down. Now. No more killing the living, not today." The snipers hesitated, then slowly lowered their weapons. Derek stepped forward, the weight of the day visible in his stance.

Bellamy joined him, both men locking eyes in a silent understanding.

They shook hands, firm, respectful.

"Good luck with Ellis," Derek said gruffly.

Bellamy nodded. "Thanks. And once this is over, I hope Kinross and New Haven can finally be friends."

With that, the groups separated. Bellamy and his team disappeared toward Kinross, their faces set with grim determination. Derek's group loaded back into the van, turning toward New Haven, their home base, and the uncertain peace that awaited.

As Bellamy pulled up to Kinross, the gates clattered open. Soldiers manned the towers above, rifles trained on the vehicle, but they didn't fire. Ellis stood just beyond the threshold, arms crossed, expression unreadable.

"It's been three weeks," Ellis snapped as the truck rolled to a halt. "Where the hell have you been?"

Bellamy stepped out slowly, his eyes burning with contempt. "I've been doing what you asked. Chasing people across a wasteland, dragging them out of ruins, risking everything. We lost Raven, Ellis. Torn apart by a horde while trying to catch your goddamn specimens." His voice cracked slightly with grief. "I lost a friend today. So don't give me crap because I wasn't fast enough for your schedule."

Ellis narrowed his eyes, tone chillingly even. "We'll discuss this in my office."

Bellamy didn't respond. He just walked past him. Munroe followed quietly, glancing over his shoulder. As they crossed the inner courtyard toward the central tower, Bellamy slipped a folded note into Munroe's hand. "You know what to do," he muttered without looking back. Munroe nodded and kept walking as Bellamy ascended the tower alone.

Inside Ellis's office, Bellamy stood near the wide, grimy window overlooking the base. His thoughts raced, of Raven, of Derek, of what might be possible if he survived the next hour. The door creaked open behind him. Ellis entered slowly, flanked by five of his most loyal bodyguards, all heavily armed. He poured himself a drink, the ice clinking softly in the glass.

"You've gone soft," Ellis said casually, sipping his whisky. "I had high hopes for you. But now... I'm not sure where your loyalties lie."

Bellamy turned, meeting his gaze head-on. "My loyalty was to survival. To building something that lasts. You? You're just playing god."

Ellis chuckled darkly. "And what are you, then? The messiah?"

Bellamy gave a tight, grim smile. "Nah. Just the guy who finally decided enough was enough."

Suddenly, a distant explosion echoed from below. The entire room trembled. Ellis's eyes darted to the guards. "What the—" Before he could finish, Munroe's voice crackled over the radio on one of the guards' shoulders. "Stage one complete. Outer towers secured. The people are with us. Surrender, or fall."

Bellamy raised his hands slowly, not in surrender, but as a sign of restraint. "Don't make this harder than it has to be."

The guards looked to Ellis, waiting for an order. But for the first time, uncertainty clouded his eyes. Outside, shouting and screaming as Kinross erupted into chaos, soldiers loyal to Bellamy locked down gates, cutting power, dragging Ellis's inner circle from buildings.

The civil war had begun.

Back at New Haven. The gates groaned open as Derek's vehicle rolled in. Dust caked the windows, the engine choking as it slowed to a halt. He stepped out with urgency written all over his face, his expression hard and focused.

"We need the bus ready," he called out loudly. "Anyone able and willing to fight gear up! You've got ten minutes. Grab what weapons you can. This is happening now!" Voices erupted across the yard as the community snapped into motion.

Jennifer pushed through the crowd and ran up to him. "What's going on? What happened?"

Derek pulled her aside. "We did it. Bellamy's plan worked. The lab is gone. But he told me something just before we left... He's going back to Kinross, and when he does, it's all kicking off. Civil war. He's taking Ellis down tonight."

Jennifer's eyes widened, jaw tightening. "Then I'm not staying behind this time. I'm coming with you."

"Jennifer—" Derek starts to say but Jennifer cuts him off and says

"No. I am coming. End of."

Derek gave her a quick nod. "Alright. Let's move."

Maggie, Anne, Daryl, Lee, Bill, Steph, Vicki, David, and Ashley were already at the armory, collecting weapons, loading ammo, checking bags and radios. The bus stood in the courtyard, engine already rumbling, a dull roar beneath the mounting tension.

"Father Luke, Sarah!" Derek called. "Take Callum to medical. His leg's broken, he won't be coming with us." Father Luke nodded solemnly, helping to carry Callum into the building.

Just then, Jillian emerged from the school building, her face pale but determined. "Derek!" she called out, jogging toward him. "I need to speak to you."

"I can't, not now, Jillian," Derek said, barely slowing. "When I get back. I promise." But as he stepped onto the bus, she leaned in close, whispering something into his ear. Derek froze for half a second, his jaw clenched. Then, without responding to her, he turned to the others. "Bill, get us moving. Kinross is waiting."

As the bus lurched forward, Jennifer slid into the seat next to Derek. She looked at him suspiciously. "What did she say to you?".

Derek kept his eyes ahead. "She asked me to bring Steph back alive. Said he's special to her."

Jennifer raised an eyebrow. "That's it?"

"Yeah." He nodded, forcing a calm he didn't feel. "That's it."

But the truth sat heavy in his chest. Jillian told him that she lied about the other night. That what happened, really did happen. But he didn't have time to process this. He had some unfinished business to take care of. The bus rumbled through the gate, into the fading light, heading for the firestorm that awaited them at Kinross.

Bellamy sat in Ellis's office, his hands raised, breathing steady but tense. Across the desk, Ellis stood with quiet fury in his eyes, a pistol slowly drawn and resting on the table between them. "If I kill you now," Ellis said coldly, "your little war ends before it even begins."

Bellamy didn't flinch. "And if I kill you, your monstrous plans die with you."

Outside the office, the sounds of distant shouting and gunfire were beginning to echo through the walls. Most of Ellis's men had already joined the chaos, leaving behind only one loyal guard, now advancing toward Bellamy with his rifle raised. In a sudden blur of motion, Bellamy twisted, pulling a hidden blade from his boot. He lunged, driving the knife into the guard's neck. Blood sprayed as the man collapsed, gurgling. Ellis screamed and opened fire, unloading his pistol wildly. Bellamy ducked behind the dying guard's body, shielding himself from the hail of bullets. The click of an empty chamber echoed through the room. Bellamy dropped the corpse, grabbed the guard's fallen rifle, and returned fire.

Ellis barely escaped, diving under his desk. When Bellamy rounded the side, the office was empty. A faint hiss, then a clunk. Bellamy spotted a hidden button on the underside of the desk. He slammed it. A trapdoor creaked open, revealing a narrow metal ladder descending into darkness.

Without hesitation, Bellamy dropped down after him. Now in the bowels of Kinross, flanked by four of his remaining men, Ellis ran. Bellamy moved fast. Every hallway, every turn, brought more chaos. Gunfire roared in close quarters as Ellis's loyalists fired from shadows. Bellamy didn't hesitate, he shot through the storm. Ellis was always just a few steps ahead.

Down on ground level, Ellis burst out of the central tower, racing for the outer gates. Bellamy was right behind him, his boots slamming against blood-slick concrete. The gunfire from both sides echoed through the streets, turning Kinross into a battlefield. Ellis skidded to a halt just before the main gate. Bloodied, limping, wild-eyed, he reached into his coat and pulled out a small black device. He pressed a button.

BOOM.

The gates exploded outward in a flash of orange and steel, shrapnel tearing through the air. Smoke and dust choked the air, the blast tearing a huge hole in the wall. Debris rained down like ash. Ellis stepped forward, smug, thinking he'd won. The way was open. Kinross was his to abandon. But as the smoke cleared, Derek's team stood beyond the gate. Weapons raised.

FIRE!!!

Bullets screamed through the air. The deafening roar of gunfire erupted as Derek, Jennifer, Maggie, Daryl, Bill and the others cut down Ellis's final guards. One by one, they fell in the storm of bullets. Blood soaking into the rubble, bodies twitching and then still. Only Ellis remained. Bellamy emerged from the rear, blood on his sleeves, fury in his eyes. His men surrounded Ellis, rifles aimed.

Derek stepped forward. "It's over, Ellis. You've lost."

Ellis looked around at the bodies, the guns, the ruined gate. His eyes landed on Derek. "I can see your gun, Derek," he hissed. "One bullet left." He smirked. "Make it count." Then, with a laugh, Ellis raised his pistol and fired.

BANG.

Derek screamed. "NO!"

Chapter 27 – The Aftermath of War

"One bullet left, Derek... make it count," Ellis snarled, lifting his pistol with a cruel smile.

BANG!

Jennifer screamed as the bullet tore into her shoulder, knocking her sideways. She staggered, blood blooming across her shirt. "Jennifer!" Derek shouted, heart pounding in his chest. Without hesitation, Derek lunged at Ellis, tackling him to the ground. The pistol clattered away as Derek's fists rained down mercilessly on Ellis's face. Blow after blow, raw, angry, desperate. Ellis tried to shield himself, but Derek's fury was unstoppable. Finally, when his arms ached and his breath came ragged, Derek stepped back, gasping. Ellis lay broken and bleeding, barely conscious. Derek retrieved his pistol, raised it slowly.

BANG.

Ellis's head snapped back. Bullet to the head. The fight was over. Jennifer collapsed to the ground, clutching her shoulder, pain and fear etched on her face.

Derek rushed to her side, dropping to his knees. "We're not losing you too," he whispered fiercely.

The others scrambled, Maggie kneeled beside Jennifer, pulling out bandages, Daryl shouting for calm, Bill and Lee moving to help. Bellamy watched silently, eyes hard but respectful.

Derek looked up, voice hoarse but determined. "No more blood for Ellis. No more war."

He lowered his pistol, the weight of everything crashing down around them. Derek held Jennifer's hand tightly as Maggie pressed against the wound, trying desperately to slow the bleeding. Jennifer's face was pale, sweat beading on her forehead.

"She's losing a lot of blood," Maggie said quietly, her voice tight with worry. "It's a bad wound... I'm not sure if she'll make it."

Derek's heart clenched. "No, Jen, stay with me. You're going to pull through. You have to."

Jennifer's eyes fluttered, and she squeezed his hand weakly. "Derek... I'm scared."

He swallowed hard, forcing himself to stay calm. "I'm right here. We're going to get you help. You're stronger than this."

Bellamy moved quickly, rallying the others. "We have to move. Now. If she stays here, she won't survive."

Bill and Lee gathered stretchers and supplies while Daryl kept watch for any threats. Derek refused to leave Jennifer's side, holding her hand as they carefully lifted her onto the stretcher.

Maggie continued to work, but her face was grim. "She's fighting, but we need a doctor, and fast." As they made their way to the vehicles, the heavy silence between the group spoke volumes. The cost of victory was now painfully clear.

Bellamy placed a firm hand on Derek's shoulder. "We'll get through this. Together."

Derek nodded, though inside the fear gnawing at him felt relentless. Jennifer's breathing was shallow, but she managed a faint smile. "We'll see tomorrow," she whispered. Derek promised himself he'd make sure she did.

The bus moved fast, tires kicking up dust and gravel as the vehicles tore down the rough roads back toward New Haven. Inside the back of the bus, Jennifer lay on the stretcher, pale and fragile, her breathing shallow but steady. Maggie sat beside her, applying pressure to the wound, whispering encouragement.

Derek stayed close, never letting go of Jennifer's hand, his eyes locked on her face as if willing her to hold on. "We're almost there," he said, voice tight with hope and fear.

At the front of the bus, the others sat tensely, their faces marked by exhaustion and worry. Jennifer's injury had shaken them all. Anne wiped tears silently, while Erin and Lee prepared the medical area ahead. Father Luke sat quietly, murmuring prayers for Jennifer's survival. When the bus finally pulled into New Haven, a small medical team awaited, ready to take Jennifer inside. Derek helped lift her carefully, feeling the weight of every heartbeat as they moved quickly into the makeshift infirmary.

Maggie and Erin worked swiftly, administering fluids, prepping for surgery. Derek paced anxiously just outside the doors. Hours passed, the ticking clock stretching unbearably. Finally, Erin emerged, exhaustion plain on her face. "She's stable for now," Erin said cautiously. "We did everything we could, but it's critical. We need to monitor her closely over the next 48 hours."

Derek nodded, relief flooding through him yet tempered by the uncertainty. He took Jennifer's hand again, brushing her hair back gently. "Stay with us, Jen," he whispered. "We're not done fighting."

Outside the infirmary, the group gathered, the weight of loss and hope mingling in the tense air. Jennifer's fight had become their fight and none of them would give up.

"Empty the bus and the truck." Daryl ordered. "We need to move fast."

As the bus and truck rumbled back towards Kinross, the weight of the day's bloodshed pressed down on everyone. Derek's broken spirit was mirrored in the hollow silence of the survivors. Callum's injury left Daryl stepping up without hesitation, his voice steady but heavy.

Bill took the truck while Daryl took the wheel of the bus, each carrying the battered remnants of what once was a fighting force. The destruction at Kinross was stark, makeshift barriers of overturned cars, tables, anything they could throw together to seal the breach Ellis had made. Bellamy exhaled deeply, relief mixing with exhaustion. Daryl pulled the bus to a stop right at the ruined gates.

"Get everyone on, Bellamy," Daryl said. "There's not much time. The dead would have heard that explosion and gun fire, every freak within 50 miles will be on their way."

One by one, the survivors clambered between the bus and truck, weary and bloodied but alive. Bellamy's voice broke the silence. "Fifty-four... that's all. Fifty-four of over one seventy people."

Daryl placed a steadying hand on Bellamy's shoulder. "Don't blame yourself. All of this was Ellis' doing."

As they neared New Haven, the battered gates came into view, a grim reminder of all they had fought for. The bus slowed and came to a halt. Bellamy, tired but resolute, ordered every weapon handed over to Steph and Ross. "I mean all weapons. No exceptions." His people complied quietly, the gravity of surrender sinking in.

Daryl stepped forward. "We'll set you up in A-block. Food and water will be provided. The cameras will be active. I won't lock the external gate to the yard, but the internal one will be locked with a guard posted."

Bellamy nodded slowly. "I would've done the same."

A fragile peace had been forged, born from loss and necessity. But beneath it all, the question remained, how long could this uneasy alliance hold?

Jillian found Derek sitting alone amid the chaos, his face a mask of pain and exhaustion. Without a word, she sat beside him, their shoulders brushing. Tears streamed down their faces, raw and unspoken grief hanging heavy between them.

Maggie approached quietly, her voice gentle but firm. "Come on, you two. Let's get you into the old guard sleepover room. You need to rest."

They followed her through the dim corridors, settling into the small, dusty room once used for overnight shifts. But neither Derek nor Jillian could find sleep. Their minds raced, thoughts tangled in fear and hope. What if Jennifer doesn't make it?

Hours passed in silence, until exhaustion finally claimed them both, dragging them into a restless sleep. When morning came, Maggie slipped quietly into the room. Her face was grave, but she tried to keep her voice steady. "Jennifer's still with us.. she's fighting hard. She's lost a lot of blood, and we don't have the means to replace it. She's stable for now, but.. honestly, I don't know how this will go." Derek and Jillian exchanged a glance, the weight of uncertainty settling deeper in their hearts. Derek sat up slowly, his back aching from the stiff cot. Jillian remained beside him, her hands clenched in her lap, eyes distant.

"Can I see her?" Derek asked, his voice hoarse.

Maggie hesitated, then nodded. "Briefly. She's sedated, but.. it might help. Just don't stay too long."

Derek rose without a word, moving through the corridor like a ghost. The halls of New Haven, once a place of routine and rebuilding, now felt haunted by the echoes of war and loss. He entered the infirmary. Jennifer lay pale and still, a bandage wrapped tightly around her shoulder, stained a deep crimson. Machines improvised from salvaged tech beeped quietly beside her, their sounds more fragile than comforting.

He took her hand gently. It felt cold. "I'm here," he whispered, crouching beside her. "I'm so sorry.. this wasn't supposed to happen."

She didn't stir, but her fingers twitched faintly, whether from pain or recognition, he couldn't tell. He rested his forehead against her hand, holding back the tide of emotion that threatened to drown him. Jillian appeared in the doorway a few minutes later. She didn't speak, just stood silently, watching.

Maggie returned and touched Derek's shoulder. "She needs rest. So do you." He nodded and stood, glancing at Jennifer one last time before following Jillian back out.

That evening, New Haven felt eerily quiet. The survivors from Kinross sat silently in A-Block, eating rationed meals, trauma etched into every line of their faces. Children clung to parents, and some stared blankly into the distance. In the council room, Daryl, Maggie, Steph, and Ross gathered to discuss what came next. Bellamy joined them reluctantly, guilt still etched deep into his expression.

"We'll need to integrate them slowly," Daryl said. "Assign work, rotate patrols. But we can't pretend things are fine."

Bellamy spoke up, voice low. "We lost everything because of one man's ambition. That doesn't excuse what I did before. But I want to make it right.. if you'll let me."

Silence followed. Then Maggie nodded. "You can start by helping clean up the wall breach tomorrow."

Back in the sleepover room, Derek sat on the edge of the cot, staring at the floor. Jillian approached and sat beside him once more."You never told Jennifer the truth," she said softly.

Derek didn't look at her. "She's the one I love." he said,

"I know," Jillian replies, the corners of her mouth tightening. "I just wanted you to know that if she doesn't make it... I'll be here. Not in the way you might think. Just here."

Derek finally turned to her, pain clouding his eyes. "I don't know how to move forward from this."

"You don't," Jillian replied. "You just take the next breath. Then the one after."

The two sat together in silence again, broken, waiting, and clinging to the hope that the woman who meant the world to them both would open her eyes.

Later that night, the quiet hum of New Haven was broken only by the faint sounds of wind brushing past the half-repaired walls. A low rain began to fall, tapping gently on the windows. Inside the old sleepover room, Derek paced in the dim light while Jillian sat, arms wrapped around her knees. Maggie appeared again in the doorway, her eyes weary but alert. Derek froze.

"She's awake," Maggie said quietly.

He rushed past her without a word. Jennifer blinked against the weak overhead light, her skin pale, her breaths shallow. Her eyes found Derek as he entered, and for a long second they just looked at each other. Then her lips curved faintly. "You always come back to me," she whispered.

Derek dropped to his knees beside her, tears already falling again. He took her hand gently. "Always. You scared the hell out of me."

Jennifer gave a soft, pained laugh. "Yeah... Well, I didn't exactly plan it."

"You're going to be okay," he said, almost as if trying to convince himself.

She didn't respond to that. Instead, she squeezed his hand. "Did we win?"

He hesitated, then nodded. "Yeah. Ellis is gone. Kinross is gone too, mostly... only fifty-four survivors."

Jennifer closed her eyes for a moment. "Too many lost. For what?"

"For peace," he said softly. "At least... I hope so." He leaned forward and kissed her forehead. She smiled faintly before drifting back into sleep.

The next morning brought grey skies and the scent of ash lingering in the air. Bellamy was already outside at the wall breach, sleeves rolled up, hauling scrap metal into place. A few of his people worked alongside New Haven's own. Tension was still present, but there was no yelling, no threats, just tired cooperation. Inside, the council had reconvened.

"We need a new structure," Maggie said. "No more factions. No more titles. One community."

Daryl nodded. "We rebuild together. Bellamy's people get the same rations, same rules. No power games. That's over."

Steph added, "We'll monitor for any lingering loyalty to Ellis. But for now, it's unity or nothing."

Derek entered quietly, a different man than the one who had led them to war. Jennifer was stable, and that seemed to have lit a faint fire inside him again. "Jennifer's going to make it," he announced. The room visibly relaxed.

Bellamy stood. "Then I say we start again. Together. Not just with words. But action."

Maggie extended her hand across the table. Bellamy hesitated, then took it.

Outside, in the courtyard, children began to play with sticks like swords. A sign of peace, or just innocent ignorance, either way, it was something. Inside, Derek stepped out into the hallway, finding Jillian nearby.

"She's awake," he told her.

Jillian smiled softly. "Good."

They stood silently for a while, side by side, watching as people moved about, fixing, building, helping. The war had ended. The healing had just begun. With Jennifer stable, for now, Derek stepped out of the infirmary, drained but determined. His heart was still in that room with her, but the rest of him had work to do.

In the main meeting room of A-Block, he gathered the remaining council members: Daryl, Callum, Jillian, Lee, Maggie and Anne. He also asked Bellamy and Munroe to join them, no longer outsiders, but potential leaders in a new future. As the group took their seats, Derek stood.

"We've lost a lot," he began, his voice calm but heavy. "More than most people should in one lifetime. But if we've learned anything, it's that division only weakens us. We fought a war to end tyranny, not to carry on old grudges." He looked directly at Bellamy and Munroe. "That's why I'm proposing this, there's no more people from New Kinross and New Haven. We are just one community, one people. And to show that trust goes both ways, if no one here objects... I want to add Bellamy and Munroe to the council."

Silence. Then Callum shifted in his seat and gave a nod. "Works for me," he said. "They bled for this, just like we did."

"I agree," Jillian added. "We can't keep rebuilding with walls between us."

Daryl followed. "They stood with us when it counted."

Lee and Anne exchanged a glance and nodded as well. Derek turned back to Bellamy and Munroe.

"You're not outsiders anymore."

Bellamy stood, clearly caught off guard. "I didn't fight this war to end up back in charge," he said plainly.

Before anyone could respond, Daryl leaned back in his chair with a smirk. "You're not," he said. "Our fearless leader is Derek." A light chuckle rippled through the room.

Derek gave Daryl a side glance, trying not to smile. "Inside joke," Derek said dryly. "Just ignore him." Even Bellamy cracked a faint grin. Munroe shook his head with a rare smile of his own and stepped forward, shaking Derek's hand firmly. The room shifted into quiet conversation and discussions about food stores, medical supplies and rebuilding trust.

Outside, survivors cleaned debris and shared bread. The dead had taken much. But the living, what few remained, were already taking the first steps toward something better. Inside, Derek lingered by the window until Jillian approached, quiet as ever. Her face was tired, like his, but her eyes held something more.

"She's still fighting," Jillian said. "Jennifer. She's weak, but.. she's still here."

Derek nodded, voice low. "So we fight too. For her. For all of them."

He didn't know what tomorrow would bring. But for tonight, at least, he had hope. And for now, that was enough. As Jillian stepped forward, quietly asking Derek for a reassuring hug, the door to the room slammed open.

"Derek, come quick it's Jennifer!" Maggie called, her face pale, eyes wide with panic. Without hesitation, the three of them sprinted through the corridor toward the infirmary. The sound of machines beeping wildly grew louder with each step. Inside, Jennifer lay still on the bed, her skin flushed, sweat beading along her brow. The monitor beside her screamed with erratic alerts. "She's spiked a temperature," Maggie said, breathless and panicked, checking Jennifer's vitals. "She might have an infection. Her wound could be going septic. And all we've got are tablet-based antibiotics. I've been trying to crush and dissolve them into water, but I don't know if it's enough. It's not working fast enough."

Derek moved to her side, grabbing Jennifer's hand, it was burning hot to the touch. Her breathing was shallow, strained.

"Where would I find IV antibiotics?" he asked, desperation edging into his voice. "We need something stronger, faster."

Maggie looked at him grimly. "A hospital. Your best bet would need to be a proper hospital, but..."

She didn't need to finish the sentence. They all knew the truth. Hospitals were ground zero when the outbreak began. Packed with chaos. Patients. Panic. Death. And now? zombie nests.

"Anywhere local?" Daryl asked, having just entered after overhearing the tail end. "Any hospital close enough?"

"There's Hairmyres Hospital just east of East Kilbride," Maggie replied, "but that place... I can't even imagine what it looks like now."

Derek looked down at Jennifer. Her face was twitching slightly, unconscious, drifting between worlds. He gritted his teeth. "I'm going," he said. "I'll get what we need."

"I'll come with you," Daryl said instantly.

Maggie turned back toward her medical table. "You'll need a list. I'll write down everything you are looking for, flucloxacillin, ceftriaxone, saline bags, syringes, IV lines."

"You're not going alone," Jillian added firmly. "Not this time."

Derek looked at her, then nodded. "Gear up," he said. "We move in thirty." And just like that, the fight wasn't over. It had only just begun again, this time, against the clock.

Chapter 28: The Hospital

The tension hung thick in the air as the group gathered at the New Haven gate, checking weapons, loading ammo, and reviewing Maggie's handwritten list one more time. Derek tightened the strap on his rifle as he stepped toward the vehicle. From behind, Bellamy and Ortega approached at a steady pace, both armed and ready.

"Let us come with you," Bellamy said, his tone calm but resolute.

"I want to help." Ortega nodded beside him. "And I need to feel like I'm doing something. Anything."

Derek studied them for a moment, then gave a nod. "Alright. We move in ten." With a shared glance of understanding, Bellamy and Ortega hurried to gather their kits.

Ten minutes later, the car rolled through the New Haven gate, stretching out toward the grey, broken horizon. The road ahead was cracked and empty, silence clinging to the world like fog. Derek gripped the steering wheel, his jaw tight, eyes scanning the road ahead. Jillian sat beside him in the passenger seat, double-checking the map and marking the route toward East Kilbride. Behind them, Daryl, Bellamy, and Ortega sat in the back, each lost in their thoughts. Nobody spoke much. There wasn't a lot left to say.

The closer they got to Hairmyres Hospital, the heavier the air became. Even from a distance, the structure loomed like a haunted monument to the old world, windows shattered, parts of the upper floors burned out, the overgrown car park packed tight with rusting ambulances and long-abandoned vehicles.As they pulled up to the hospital perimeter, Derek killed the engine. All five stepped out slowly, weapons raised. "Eyes open," he whispered. "We get in, we get what we need, we get out."

Bellamy looked toward the broken entrance. "There's no way this place is empty." Ortega scanned the shadowed hallways through the smashed front doors.

"Which means it's going to be crawling." Jillian exhaled, gripping her sidearm. "Let's just find the meds and get back before things go to hell."

Daryl nodded. "We split into two groups, me and Ortega take the pharmacy wing, Derek, Jillian, and Bellamy go after the IV supplies."

Derek nodded in agreement. "No heroics. Keep radios close. If anything moves… drop it."

The teams split and disappear into the shadow-choked corridors of the dead hospital, unaware of the nightmare that lay waiting deep within its walls. Derek, Jillian, and Bellamy moved cautiously down the dark, debris-strewn hallway, the beam of Jillian's flashlight slicing through the darkness. The air was thick with mildew and the distant stench of decay. Every footstep echoed like a scream. They reached a rusted sign half-hanging from a broken mount:

"SUPPLY STORAGE – WARD 3B →"

"This way," Derek said in a hushed voice, taking point. Bellamy covered the rear while Jillian kept to Derek's side, scanning every corner, every doorway. The silence was unnatural, the kind of stillness that screamed of ambush. They passed overturned gurneys and bloodied smocks, old wheelchairs frozen mid-roll. On the walls, handprints and smears of red told stories of panic and tragedy long since ended.

"I hate hospitals," Bellamy muttered.

"You and everyone else," Jillian whispered.

They turned the final corner and found a locked steel door marked "Medical Storage – Authorized Personnel Only." Derek knelt by the lock, examining it.

"Mechanical. Might still give," he said, pulling out a pry bar.

"Let me try," Bellamy offered, setting his rifle against the wall and taking the tool. With a grunt, he wedged it into the seam and forced it hard. The lock gave way with a sharp metallic crack, echoing down the corridor like a gunshot.

They froze.

Silence.

Then, a low moan, distant. Then another. And another.

"We need to move, now," Derek said, pushing the door open. Inside, the room was dusty but relatively intact. Rows of shelves lined the walls, stocked with faded boxes and cracked plastic tubs. Jillian rushed to the nearest shelf and scanned labels.

"Got them!" she said, grabbing two packs of IV antibiotics and stuffing them in her satchel. "And more over here, bottles, syringes, bags."

As they collected what they could carry, a sound came from the hallway, the dragging scrape of feet. Derek turned toward the door. "Time's up. Let's go!" Jillian slung her bag over her shoulder. "Let's go!" Derek repeated They pushed out into the corridor, three zombies rounding the far end, followed by more shadows shifting in the dark.

"Go, GO !" Bellamy shouted, raising his rifle and taking a shot, one zombie dropped. Derek fired his pistol, another down.

"Back to the front doors" Derek barked. "We regroup with Daryl and Ortega at the entrance!"

They sprinted down the hallway, boots pounding, breath ragged. As they rounded the corner, more zombies spilled from side rooms, drawn by the noise.

Bellamy shouted, "Left! This way!" They crashed through an old ward door and out into a side corridor, dodging past wheelchairs and overturned beds.

Derek keyed his radio: "Daryl! We're pinned near ward 3B, what's your status?!"

A burst of static, then Daryl's voice: "We've got what we need, circle around, back exit's clear, we'll cover you!"

Derek looked at the others. "Back exit. Let's move!"

Meanwhile outside the emergency entrance, Daryl and Ortega stood over a pile of scavenged supplies they'd already loaded into a cart,IV fluid bags, tubing, gloves, disinfectant, and more. The area was quiet, for now. The dead seemed to have left this wing. Daryl popped the cap on a bottle of water and passed it to Ortega.

"Not bad for a suicide run." Ortega gave a half-smirk.

"Still breathing. I'll take the win." Daryl replied, Just then, the radio on his hip crackled violently, Derek's voice coming through, ragged and strained: "Daryl! We're pinned near ward 3B, what's your status" Daryl replies "Circle around to the back of the hospital, the exit's clear, we'll cover you!"

Daryl instantly clipped the radio to his vest and grabbed his rifle. "That's our cue."

"Let's move," Ortega said, already hauling one of the bags toward the rear of the building. They sprinted around the hospital's west side, ducking under collapsed fencing and navigating old parking lot wreckage. The muffled echo of gunshots rolled from inside the structure, Derek's team fighting their way out.

Ortega raised his rifle, scanning the rear exit door. "Clear, so far."

A moment later, the rear door burst open, and Derek stumbled through first, blood splattered on his arms, followed by Jillian, clutching her bag tight, and Bellamy, covering the rear with bursts of rifle fire.

"Let's go!" Derek shouted, not stopping. Ortega fired two quick shots into zombies gaining from behind. Daryl stepped in, pulling Jillian toward the truck.

Bellamy slammed the door behind them, and the group tore off toward the vehicles. Zombies spilled from the hospital entrance, groaning, arms reaching but they were already peeling out of the lot, tires screeching on cracked tarmac.

Inside the truck, Derek clutched the antibiotic pack like gold. "We got it," he said, breathless.

"Let's just hope we're not too late," Jillian murmured, eyes focused on the horizon as the hospital vanished behind them. The road stretched endlessly behind them, East Kilbride now just a ghost in the rearview mirror. New Haven lay ahead, close, but not close enough. The truck had been humming steadily for most of the return journey, but as they reached a narrow bend flanked by old woodland, it gave a violent clunk, then shuddered. "What's that?" Jillian asked, sitting upright.

Bellamy, behind the wheel, swore under his breath. "Something's not right—"

The vehicle lurched, coughed, and finally gave out with a mechanical wheeze. Silence followed, broken only by the settling creaks of the engine. Derek was already stepping out, boots crunching gravel. Daryl popped the hood, and steam hissed into the cool air.

"Damn," Derek muttered, leaning in. "Same pipe as before. It's split clean down the middle."

Daryl slammed the hood down in frustration. "We've patched it twice already. No tools, no sealant. We're not fixing it here."

A heavy pause settled over the group. The quiet stretch of road suddenly felt hostile, exposed. Ortega stepped forward, adjusting his pack.

"Then we walk. Best get moving, double time back home." Everyone turned to look at him. He blinked. "What?"

Daryl smirked, a soft chuckle escaping him. "You said 'home.' First time I've heard you say that."

Bellamy raised an eyebrow, smiling faintly. Jillian glanced over at Derek, who just nodded, the corners of his mouth lifting despite the tension. Ortega looked around, awkwardly scratching the back of his neck. "Yeah, well... I guess it's growing on me."

Derek clapped a hand on his shoulder. "Let's get moving before we end up part of the scenery."

With the sun beginning its descent, casting long shadows across the road, the group shouldered their packs and set off at a brisk pace, New Haven waiting at the end of the line, and Jennifer, still fighting, waiting for the medicine that might just save her.

Back in New Haven, the air inside the infirmary was heavy with tension. The soft beeping of the monitoring machines and the occasional groan from the wounded were the only sounds that filled the space. Jennifer lay still, her breathing shallow, her skin flushed with fever. Maggie sat beside her, a cloth in hand, gently dabbing sweat from her forehead. A row of half-crushed antibiotic tablets lined the table, dissolved in water and administered in hopes of helping, but so far, they hadn't made much difference. I hope they're back soon, Maggie thought grimly. They have to be. The door creaked open. Abby stepped in, her presence quiet but purposeful.

"How is everything?" she asked, glancing around, then settling her eyes on Jennifer. Maggie hesitated. She still wasn't sure how much to trust Abby or the others from Kinross. Old loyalties didn't disappear overnight.

"She's… holding on," Maggie finally said. "But the meds aren't helping like I hoped."

Abby walked closer, her voice soft but steady. "I used to be a herbalist. Before all this," she said, gesturing faintly to the world outside. "I know of a few wild plants that can act like antibiotics. If I had permission to go out, I might be able to make something stronger, more natural."

Maggie considered it. "You'd risk going out there… for her?"

Abby didn't hesitate. "She's one of us now, isn't she?" There was a long pause, then a slight nod from Maggie.

"Your best bet is to speak to Callum. Derek put him in charge while he's away."

"I'll do that. Thank you, Maggie," Abby said, already turning toward the door. As she left, Maggie turned her gaze back to Jennifer, brushing a strand of hair from her face. "Hold on a bit longer, love. They're out there doing everything they can." She glanced at the crushed pills on the tray again. And maybe... just maybe, help is closer than we think.

Meanwhile in New Haven's command center, early afternoon. The hum of the generator and distant voices echoed through the hallways of the former prison turned sanctuary. Callum sat at the old security desk, leg propped up in a splint, a radio in one hand and a growing pile of notes in the other. His face was tired, worn from both pain and responsibility, but his eyes were alert. A soft knock came at the open door. He looked up. Abby stood there, hands folded in front of her.

"Sorry to disturb you."

Callum gestured her in. "You're not. Come in. Is everything all right?"

She stepped in slowly. "It's Jennifer. Maggie's been doing what she can, but the antibiotics we have aren't helping. Her fever's not breaking."

Callum's jaw tightened. "Derek and the others haven't radioed since yesterday. I know they're trying, but..." He trailed off, frustration showing on his face.

"I want to help," Abby said firmly. "Before the outbreak, I studied herbal medicine. If I can get outside the gates, I might be able to find what we need, something with strong enough properties to fight the infection."

Callum studied her for a moment. "That's a big risk."

"I know. But so is waiting and doing nothing."

He nodded slowly. "Do you have a list of what you need?"

"I do," she said, pulling a folded piece of paper from her pocket and handing it over. Callum looked over it, a mix of names he recognized and others he didn't. "Alright," he said finally. "I'll approve it. But you're not going alone."

She looked relieved but curious. "Who then?"

"I'll send Vicki and David with you. They've got good eyes and steady aim. You find what you need, they'll make sure you get back in one piece."

Abby nodded gratefully. "Thank you, Callum. I'll get ready right away."

He gave her a small, strained smile. "Be careful out there, Abby. Jennifer... She means a lot to a lot of people."

"I understand," Abby said quietly. Then she turned and left, her heart pounding, not from fear, but from hope.

The gates of New Haven creaked open just enough for the three of them to slip through. Vicki took the lead, rifle slung over her shoulder and her eyes constantly scanning the treeline. David, quiet and solid, stayed close to Abby, his shotgun resting in his hands. Abby carried only a small satchel and a folding knife on her belt. Her weapon was her knowledge and today, she needed that more than ever. The forest was quieter than usual, the undead drawn away by past events. But none of them let their guard down.

"Are you sure this is the best spot?" Vicki asked in a low voice, adjusting her grip as they followed a narrow deer path deeper into the woods.

Abby nodded. "There's a natural spring about two miles in, and the soil there tends to grow the things I'm looking for: goldenseal, echinacea, elderberry… if I'm lucky, maybe even some wild garlic."

David glanced at her. "You really think this stuff will work?"

"I think it's her best shot without IV meds," Abby said firmly. "I've treated infections before, some bad. It won't be perfect, but it might give her a fighting chance."

They moved in silence after that, the tension in the air thick, but not hostile. Focused. Vicki motioned for them to stop as they reached a rocky outcrop, kneeling to check the area. No movement. No sounds beyond wind and birds. "All clear," she whispered.

Abby moved ahead, crouching near a patch of shade beneath a fallen tree. Her eyes lit up. "This is it," she said quickly, pulling gloves from her pack. "Goldenseal." As she began carefully pulling roots and trimming leaves, David stood with his back to her, watching the path they came from. Vicki took the perimeter. Minutes passed, then Abby called out again. "Found elderberry too!" She quickly gathered what she could, tucking it all safely in her satchel. Suddenly, Vicki whistled softly, two short bursts. David and Abby froze. That was the signal for movement.

Vicki emerged from behind a bush, crouched low. "Two zombies heading this way. Slow ones. We can move out without a fight if we're quick."

"Got what I need," Abby whispered, closing the flap on her bag.

They retraced their steps swiftly but quietly, sticking to brush and low ground. The zombies never even saw them. By the time New Haven's walls were back in view, the sun was starting to dip low on the horizon. As the gates opened again, Callum stood there, one crutch under his arm. Relief washed over his face when he saw them safe.

Abby approached first. "I got what I needed," she said, holding up her satchel. "I'll start making it right away."

"Good work," Callum said. "Now go save her."

The sun dipped lower behind the hills, casting long, stretched shadows across the cracked tarmac of the forgotten road. Derek's boots crunched gravel with every heavy step. His legs ached, but it wasn't pain that fueled him, it was Jennifer. She needed them back. Needed what they'd risked everything to find. Every few hundred yards, they checked another vehicle. Each one was the same, useless. Either stripped, dead, or wrecked. Hope drained a little more each time the door creaked open and revealed another pile of dust and rust.

"We've been walking for hours," Ortega muttered, wiping sweat from his brow. "Feels like we've done ten miles already."

"We've still got around eight," Bellamy grumbled. "At this rate, we'll get there tomorrow night. We need to find somewhere. Just for tonight."

"No," Derek said sharply, not even turning around. "We keep going. I don't care if it's all night." Bellamy sighed but didn't argue. Not yet. They trudged on another mile or so until Daryl suddenly grabbed Derek by the arm and spun him around.

"Don't be stupid," he snapped. "You've got bloodshot eyes, your legs are shaking, and you're talking like sleep doesn't matter. You know what's out there, forest, towns, blind corners. You want us to walk into that",

For a second, it looked like he might explode. But instead, he just stood there, chest heaving, face torn in frustration. He didn't want to stop. Couldn't. Not while she lay in that bed fighting for her life.

The silence hung heavy for a moment before Bellamy softly added, "Just a few hours. We rest. Then at first light, we move. If you're falling apart, the rest of us will too."

The group stood at a crossroads, literally and figuratively, before Derek finally gave a small nod. "Alright," he murmured. "We stop." Ortega pointed toward a cluster of buildings just off the road.

"Looks like an old rest stop. Maybe we'll find something dry."

The team made their way off the road and into the small complex. A battered diner and a few boarded-up shops stood still against the approaching darkness. The place was eerily quiet, but it would have to do. Inside the diner, overturned chairs and broken glass littered the floor. Derek sat in the corner near a cracked window, his pack still on his back, his shoulders slumped. He didn't speak. Just stared out toward the road they still had to walk. Bellamy and Ortega took watch by the doors. Daryl cleared a corner and sat with his back against the wall, crossbow in his lap.

"A few hours," Derek whispered to himself. "Then we move."

The moon hung , casting a pale light through the shattered diner window. The world outside was still, but Derek's thoughts were anything but. He sat by the door, rifle across his lap, eyes scanning the darkness, though nothing stirred beyond the broken parking lot.

Behind him, the others lay in uneasy slumber. Bellamy was propped against the counter, Ortega curled near the far booth, and Daryl rested with one eye half-open. It was quiet, but the silence only made Derek's anxiety louder. He hadn't slept, not really, not since Jennifer was shot. His mind wouldn't let him. Every time he closed his eyes, he pictured Jennifer, pale, sweating, slipping further away. Footsteps padded softly on the cracked tiles. Jillian appeared beside him, wrapping a blanket around her shoulders. She eased herself down next to him, nudging his arm gently.

"You all right?" she asked softly. He didn't answer at first. His jaw clenched, eyes fixed on the moonlit road. Finally, he whispered,

"No. But I need to be."

"I'm sure she will be fine," Jillian says, her voice warm and steady. "You don't have to be strong, not all the time. I'm here, Derek. As your friend... your sister-in-law... someone you can count on. Always."

He gave a faint smile but didn't look at her. "I keep thinking... What if she dies while I'm out here? What if I lose her and I'm not there to say goodbye? What if Maggie can't do anything? What then, Jill?" She didn't answer right away. Instead, she rested her head gently against his shoulder, letting the silence hold them. After a few moments, Derek spoke again, quieter this time. "I remember what you whispered before we left for Kinross." Jillian shifted slightly, her heart catching in her chest. "You told me you knew what happened a few days ago" Derek said. "Said you hoped I didn't die... and that you'd see me real soon."

Jillian looked down, her voice barely audible. "I meant every word."

"I know," Derek replied. "And I didn't die. But now... I feel like I'm losing everything anyway."

Jillian reached out and took his hand, her grip firm and reassuring. "Then fight, Derek. Fight like hell. For her. For yourself. For all of us."

He finally turned his head to meet her eyes. In the low light, there was something raw and broken behind his gaze, but also something resolute. "I will," he said. "I swear I will." They sat together in silence, side by side as the night crept on and the promise of dawn lingered just over the horizon.

The infirmary was quiet, save for the rhythmic beeping of the machines beside Jennifer's bed. Abby stood over a small table near the corner, her hands steady as she completed the mixture. The herbal antibiotic was finally blended into a saline bag—her last hope to help the woman clinging to life. She carried it over to Maggie, who quickly took it and attached it to the IV stand. With careful fingers, Maggie hooked it up and adjusted the machine settings, watching as the pale green liquid began to drip slowly into Jennifer's bloodstream.

"I hope this works," Maggie muttered under her breath, watching the IV like it held all the answers.

"So do I," Abby replied, her tone hushed but full of hope. They both stood in silence for a few seconds, watching Jennifer's chest rise and fall. Still alive. Still fighting.

The night had passed slowly. Derek hadn't slept, but the quiet had given him space to think, space he hadn't wanted, but needed. Jillian had fallen asleep beside him during their talk. At some point, she'd leaned against him, and now her head rested gently on his lap. He hadn't moved, just let her stay there, letting the warmth of another soul ease his anxious heart. As the first rays of sunlight filtered through the dust-smeared windows, Derek gently brushed her hair back and whispered,

"Jill... wake up." She stirred slowly, blinking the sleep from her eyes.

"is it Morning?" she asked.

He nodded. "Yeah. We need to move." She sat up, stretching slightly, and gave him a soft look, no words, just silent support.

Derek stood and nudged the others awake one by one. Bellamy groaned as he rose from the floor, Ortega cracked his neck, and Daryl muttered something about needing a real bed. They packed quickly, quietly. The tension in the air was unspoken, they were close now, and every minute mattered. Once their gear was loaded and checked, Derek looked toward the east.

"Let's bring her home," he said. And together, they set off down the road toward New Haven, hope weighing just as heavily as their packs.

The morning light filtered through the blinds of the infirmary, casting soft rays across the room where Jennifer lay unmoving. The soft beep of the monitor remained steady but weak, her body still fighting, still holding on. Maggie sat beside her, eyes tired, fingers fidgeting nervously with the hem of her sleeve. The IV bag containing Abby's herbal antibiotic was nearly half-drained now, the liquid slowly feeding into Jennifer's system. Abby walked in quietly, holding a clipboard with notes she'd made through the night. She gave Maggie a small nod before glancing at the monitor.

"Her fever's dropped," Maggie said, voice laced with cautious optimism. "It's not gone... but it's down." Abby exhaled slowly. "That's something. It means her body's responding."

Maggie reached forward and gently brushed a few strands of hair from Jennifer's damp forehead. "Come on, Jen," she whispered. "You're not allowed to quit. Not now."

The door creaked open behind them, and Father Thomas stepped in with a flask of tea in hand. He didn't speak, just set it down by them and gave Maggie's shoulder a gentle squeeze.

"How long do you think before we'll know for sure?" Abby asked. Maggie shook her head.

"Could be hours… could be days. The infection was deep. All we can do is keep her stable and hope." Father Thomas bowed his head.

"Then we pray." The room fell quiet again. The only sounds were the IV drip, the monitor's slow rhythm, and the unspoken hope hanging heavy in the air.

The sun had barely crested the horizon, its golden glow spilling across the dew-covered fields as Derek and the group pushed forward. They were tired, hungry, sore, but the sight of the familiar hills in the distance gave them a renewed sense of urgency. Derek walked at the front, his steps relentless. Jillian stayed just behind him, occasionally glancing at his face, noting how the worry etched into every line of his expression hadn't eased since they left. Ortega had slung his rifle over his shoulder, silent but alert. Bellamy trudged along beside Daryl, exchanging quiet words, likely about repairs and logistics for what lay ahead. No one had slept much the night before, but no one complained. The only thing that mattered now was getting home.

"Another mile, maybe two," Daryl said, checking the crude map they'd drawn. "We'll be on the home stretch soon."

Derek didn't answer. His eyes were fixed on the horizon, his mind already in the infirmary, already at Jennifer's side. Every step felt like a heartbeat counting down. He needed her to be okay. He needed to get back before it was too late.

Behind him, Jillian finally broke the silence. "She's strong, Derek. Just like you. She'll hang on."

He glanced at her, and for the first time in hours, a flicker of something, hope, maybe, crossed his face. "I just need to see her," he said quietly. "I just need to see her alive." As the gates of New Haven finally appeared in the distance, the group picked up speed. Home was just ahead.

The sun had climbed higher now, casting long shadows as Derek and his group approached the gates of New Haven. From a distance, the compound looked calm, secure, even. Smoke trailed lazily from the chimney stacks. A couple of guards stood posted on the makeshift tower, rifles in hand. As the group closed in, one of the guards spotted them and raised a hand to signal. "Gates!" the guard shouted. "We've got movement, friendly!" Within moments, the gate creaked open, revealing Callum, leaning on a crutch, but standing tall, waiting beside Ross and Steph. Their faces lit up with relief as they saw the returning group.

"About bloody time," Callum said, his voice thick with emotion.

Derek didn't waste a second. He gave Callum a brief nod before pushing straight through the gate, urgency in every step. "Where is she?" he called out.

"Infirmary," Ross answered quickly. "Maggie's with her. Abby too." Jillian touched Derek's shoulder briefly before following behind him, while Daryl turned to Ross.

"We found everything, saline, IV packs, more meds than we thought we'd find."

"Good," Ross replied, grabbing one of the duffel bags. "Let's get it inside." Bellamy and Ortega trailed in last, both men taking in the familiar, now-comforting sight of New Haven.

Ortega gave a quiet grunt of satisfaction as the gates closed behind them. "It really is home now," he muttered.

As Derek disappeared into the heart of the compound, one thought repeated in his mind over and over: Please let her still be alive. Derek pushed through the doors of the infirmary, his boots echoing off the tile floor. The air was heavy, filled with the steady beep of monitors and the faint scent of antiseptic.

Maggie looked up as he entered, relief flickering in her tired eyes. She didn't even have to say anything, her expression said it all. Jennifer was still alive. Hooked up to the IV line Abby had prepared, Jennifer lay still, her face pale and slick with sweat. The antibiotics dripped slowly into her arm. Her breathing was shallow but steady.

"She spiked again about two hours ago," Maggie said softly. "But it's stabilized since we started the IV drip. It might be working."

Derek approached her bedside, his heart pounding in his ears. He sat down gently beside her, taking her hand in his, careful not to wake her. "I got what you needed," he whispered, brushing a stray strand of hair from her forehead. "I'm here."

Behind him, Jillian stood quietly, watching with a bittersweet smile. Daryl joined her at the doorway. "How's she really doing?" Daryl asked Maggie.

"Better than yesterday. But we're not out of the woods yet. If the infection doesn't break soon.." Maggie trailed off, unwilling to say the rest.

Derek just sat there, unmoving, his hand wrapped around Jennifer's. "You're strong," he whispered to her. "You've made it through everything. Just hold on a little longer."

The others left them in silence, giving him the moment. The war had ended. But the fight for Jennifer's life still hung in the balance. And for Derek... this was the battle that mattered most.

Chapter 29 – What We Have Lost

It had been four long days since Derek and the others had returned to New Haven. Four days of hope fraying at the edges. Four days of sitting by Jennifer's bedside, watching her chest rise and fall, shallow and unsteady. The IV antibiotics dripped steadily into her arm, but the fever hadn't broken. Maggie tried everything, cool compresses, herbal teas from Abby, adjusting doses, but Jennifer remained locked in a fragile limbo between life and death.

Derek sat beside her, his hands folded, eyes bloodshot from lack of sleep. He hadn't left her side except to quickly eat or stretch his legs. The rest of the group respected that space, but their worry was evident in every glance.

Maggie stood at the foot of the bed, arms crossed, frustration etched into her face. "I don't know what else to try," she finally admitted. "I've done everything I can. If the fever doesn't break soon.. her organs could start to shut down."

Derek's jaw clenched, his knuckles whitening. "No," he said quietly. "She's not dying. She's survived too much for it to end like this."

Jillian stood silently near the door, holding a damp cloth. She watched her sister's chest rise again, then fall, slow, labored. "She's always been a fighter," she whispered. "But even fighters need help."

Across New Haven, the atmosphere had shifted. The war was over, but the wounds it left behind hadn't healed. Bellamy sat near the supply depot, going over lost names. Fifty-four survivors... out of more than a hundred and seventy. Names. Faces. Friends. Ortega had taken to helping fix walls, but even he seemed quieter now, less brash, more aware of what they'd all been through. Abby worked with Maggie, preparing more herbal remedies in case they ran out of modern supplies again.

Daryl had stepped up around the compound, helping maintain calm and routine. But even he couldn't hide the tension that lingered whenever he looked toward the infirmary. They had survived the war, but New Haven was mourning.

And for Derek, all that loss meant nothing if he lost Jennifer now. He stood up slowly, leaned over the bed, and kissed her forehead. Her skin was still too hot. "I need you to come back to me," he whispered. "Please."

Outside, the wind carried the sound of distant zombies shuffling beyond the walls, a reminder that the world was still broken. But inside New Haven, everyone was holding their breath.

Waiting.

Jillian sat on the edge of her bed, the room silent but for the wind brushing against the boarded windows. Her hands trembled slightly as she laced her fingers together. Jennifer was more than a sister. She was her protector growing up, her closest confidante, and in this new world, her anchor. Jillian had whispered the truth to Derek before the battle, unsure he'd even come back. And now, watching him break piece by piece as Jennifer lay between life and death.. she didn't know how to help either of them. She hated feeling helpless.

Daryl stood on the outer perimeter wall, crossbow slung over his shoulder. He had taken more night shifts than anyone else, barely sleeping. His mind was restless. He thought about Raven. About those they'd lost. About how close Derek was to losing Jennifer. Daryl wasn't the emotional type, but he felt it, deep, gnawing grief mixed with guilt that he'd survived when so many hadn't. Still, he stayed vigilant. He figured the best thing he could do now was make sure no one else died.

Callum hobbled slightly as he walked around A-block, clipboard in hand. His leg was still mending, but he refused to be bedridden. The war had shifted something in him. Seeing the Kinross survivors broken, wounded, looking to him and Derek for structure, it lit a sense of responsibility. He was quieter now, more observant. He passed by Abby, who was drying herbs outside the infirmary, and gave her a grateful nod. She didn't need praise, but she deserved it. He glanced toward the building where Jennifer lay. Everyone was waiting, for hope, or for heartbreak.

Bellamy sat with Munroe near the remains of the burned Kinross flag they had quietly buried outside the walls. Neither of them spoke much. Bellamy stared at the darkening sky, voice quiet.

"If she doesn't make it, I don't know how Derek's going to hold this place together." Munroe nodded. "He's got people around him who care. That's more than most had."

Bellamy sighed, rubbing his face. "I just hope that's enough."

Abby was exhausted but determined. She moved between herbal mixes and Maggie's modern tools, doing what she could to bridge the gap between worlds. When the fever first spiked, she thought they were too late. But something kept Jennifer going.

"She's stronger than she looks," Abby had told Maggie. Now, every hour the woman stayed alive, Abby began to believe they might just pull her through.

Back in the infirmary, Derek sat slouched in the corner chair, eyes heavy but alert. He'd barely left the room. Jillian entered quietly, placing a cup of water on the table beside him. He didn't speak. He just reached over and took her hand. Across the room, the monitor beeped softly. One beat at a time. That's how they'd move forward.

One beat at a time.

The air in the infirmary was stale, heavy with tension and the sterile bite of alcohol and herbal tinctures. The soft beeping of the monitor had become a heartbeat for the whole of New Haven, each person silently attuned to it, as if willing Jennifer to keep fighting. Derek sat by her side, her hand clasped in both of his. Her skin still radiated warmth, but something had changed.

Her breathing, once shallow and erratic, had deepened just slightly. Not much, but enough for Maggie to take notice. She leaned over, brushing Jennifer's damp hair from her forehead, checking the IV drip again.

"I think the fever's dropping," she said softly, not daring to raise her voice in case the hope shattered.

Derek's eyes snapped up. "Are you sure?"

"I'm not sure of anything," Maggie replied, cautiously hopeful. "But she's cooler than she was this morning. Heart rate's a little more steady, and she's not as restless."

Jillian stepped in behind them, still wearing the same sweatshirt from the night before. She moved quietly to the opposite side of the bed and looked down at her sister. Jennifer's lips no longer looked as dry and cracked. Her chest rose in a smoother rhythm.

"Come on, Jen," Jillian whispered. "Stay with us."

Maggie turned to Abby, who was preparing a fresh herbal compress. "That blend you made might actually be helping."

Abby shrugged, tired but faintly smiling. "Sometimes nature surprises us. Sometimes it's just timing."

They didn't know which it was. None of them did. But for the first time in days, the fear that had clung to their throats like smoke eased, just a little. Outside, the sun was beginning to rise again, casting a soft glow over the battered walls of New Haven. Survivors were starting to emerge into the yard, moving slowly, warily, but together.

Inside the infirmary, Derek finally allowed himself a breath he hadn't taken in days. And Jennifer... her eyes fluttered once. Just for a moment. But enough. Jennifer's eyelids twitched again, a soft flicker like a whisper against the storm. Derek leaned forward, heart thudding louder than any alarm could sound. "Jen?" he said softly, barely above a whisper. "Come on... open your eyes." Jillian stepped closer, holding her breath. Then, slowly, Jennifer's eyes opened. Not fully. Just enough to show a glimpse of her hazel irises. Her gaze was unfocused, drifting toward the ceiling, then blinking slowly toward Derek.

Maggie moved in quickly, scanning the monitor, placing gentle fingers against Jennifer's wrist. Her eyes widened slightly.

"Heart rate's improving. That's good."

Jennifer's lips parted, dry and cracked. No words came, but her hand shifted just slightly in Derek's. "I'm here," he said, voice trembling now. "You're okay. Just rest."

Tears slipped silently down Jillian's face as she leaned over, gently brushing her sister's hair. "You scared the hell out of us," she whispered.

Jennifer blinked slowly, her mouth trying again. This time, a sound, soft, hoarse, escaped. "Derek..." His name. Slurred, weak, but clear enough. It hit him like a hammer to the chest. He let out a breath that cracked into a sob. "I'm here," he repeated, voice thick. "I'm not going anywhere."

Maggie nodded toward Abby, her voice a blend of relief and disbelief. "We might have turned the corner."

Later that evening word spread fast in New Haven. Whispered at first, passed from person to person like a spark in dry leaves: She's awake. By nightfall, the small infirmary was filled with silent visitors. Not crowding, just standing near the door, peeking in with hopeful eyes. Bellamy lingered outside, head bowed in quiet reflection. He'd seen more loss than most, but for once, it looked like the tide hadn't taken another. Daryl sat with Lee and Callum outside the building, each of them not speaking much, just quietly letting the moment sink in. A win. Small, fragile, but a win nonetheless.

Jennifer drifted in and out of consciousness. Each time she woke, the fog cleared a little more. Derek hadn't moved from her side. "Water," she croaked on her third awakening. Maggie was there instantly with a damp sponge, letting drops touch her lips. Jennifer groaned in discomfort but accepted it. "You're going to be okay," Jillian whispered. "Just keep fighting." Jennifer managed a small nod.

Then she looked at Derek and, for the first time in days, smiled. Only a faint curl of the lips but it was enough.

The following morning in A block it was quiet. A rare kind of quiet, the kind that follows a storm. The walls of A Block, once filled with cautious Kinross refugees, now held people who spoke in softer tones, moved with slower steps. The events of the last week had weighed heavy. In one corner, Bellamy sat with Munroe, sipping a weak coffee that Vicki had managed to scrounge together from leftover supplies. Neither spoke much. They didn't need to. The silence between them was the language of survivors. Steph passed by, his rifle slung low, nodding to them both. His walk was lighter today, and for the first time since Kinross fell, he smiled.

In the infirmary, Jennifer was asleep again, but this time, it was natural, peaceful. Derek stood at the window just inside the room, arms crossed, watching the early morning sun climb over New Haven's battered walls. Jillian brought him a blanket, still warm from the laundry room.

"She's getting better," she said.

Derek nodded. "I know."

Jillian hesitated, then leaned against the wall beside him. "You going to sleep at some point?"

"Maybe." He offered a faint smile. "I don't want to miss anything."

"You won't," Jillian said. "You saved her."

He looked down at his hands, bruised and scratched. "We all did."

Elsewhere in New Haven

Daryl and Callum walked the perimeter of the yard. Callum, using a walking stick now, was still limping but refused to be benched. "They're different," Callum said, glancing toward the Kinross folks working on reinforcing the front gates.

"Yeah," Daryl replied. "Different good, though. I think they want this to work."

"I think we all do," Callum said, pausing to rest. "Ellis... he was the worst of us. But maybe we've got a shot now."

Daryl grunted in agreement. "Still got a long road."

Callum gave him a crooked smile. "Don't we always?"

That afternoon in the courtyard. A gathering formed, not official, not planned. People just... gravitated there. Survivors from both New Haven and Kinross. They brought out chairs, crates, and sat on steps. Kids played in the dusty grass, laughter returning in short bursts. Derek finally stepped out, blinking into the light. He walked slowly, like the weight hadn't quite lifted yet. Jillian at his side. Maggie waved him over from the center of the gathering. He raised his hand in acknowledgment but didn't speak. He didn't need to. His presence alone said enough. Jennifer was alive. The fever had broken. And for now, just for now, their world held hope again.

Later that night in the infirmary. Jennifer stirred in her bed, her skin pale but no longer burning. The IV bag dripped steadily, and Maggie noted the numbers with cautious optimism. She was healing, slowly. The door creaked open. Maggie looked up, expecting Derek or Jillian. Instead, Abby stood in the doorway, clutching something wrapped in a worn towel. Her face was unreadable.

"Abby?" Maggie whispered. "You okay?" Abby nodded, stepping in slowly. She unwrapped the towel. Inside was a thin notebook, leather-bound and charred around the edges. Maggie frowned.

"I found this in the Kinross supply room before we left," Abby said. "Didn't look at it until now." She handed it over. Maggie flipped through the pages. Medical notes. Names. Dosages. But as she reached the back, something caught her eye. Coordinates. A hand-drawn map. And a familiar symbol. A double helix.

"This isn't Kinross," Maggie whispered. "This is Rose Bank."

Abby leaned in. "There was a second lab."

Maggie looked up, dread creeping in. "Another one?"

Abby nodded. "And I think... someone's still there."

Next morning in the council room

Derek stared at the notebook on the table. Jillian, Daryl, Callum, Lee, Anne, and now Bellamy and Munroe sat around him in silence. No one knew what to say.

"It could be nothing," Callum said finally. "Old records."

"Or it could be a trap," Daryl muttered.

"But what if it's not?" Jillian asked. "What if there's someone out there, someone who knows more?"

Derek's eyes hadn't left the map. "I said we were done fighting," he murmured. "But maybe this isn't a fight. Maybe this is how we win."

Bellamy exhaled slowly. "If it's Rose Bank... we've been chasing shadows. Maybe it's time we find the light."

Derek stood. "Then we go. We will finish this."

Chapter 30 – The Lab and Old Secrets

It had been a few weeks since Jennifer's fever broke.

She was alive, healing, but still too weak to sit among the others. So her place at the council table remained empty, a quiet reminder of what they almost lost.

The council sat in silence, the weight of what they were planning heavy on their shoulders. Derek stood at the head of the table, the map spread wide before them. Pins marked possible entry points, terrain obstacles, and routes in and out of the region. But one thing was certain, it wouldn't be easy.

"If it exists," Callum said finally, "this lab has been buried. Hidden deliberately."

Bellamy nodded grimly. "Ellis knew about it. That much I'm sure of now. It's where the original research started, before the outbreak."

"You think there's still someone there?" Maggie asked, her voice low.

"There might be," Bellamy replied. "But even if there's not, there could be records... answers."

Munroe leaned forward. "If we're doing this, we go quiet. No convoys, no big team. Just enough to get in, secure anything important, and get out."

Derek looked around the room.

"Then we prepare. Two days from now, we move."

Derek sat at the edge of his bed, the map from the council meeting still fresh in his mind, his thoughts clouded. The moonlight streamed faintly through the window, illuminating a room filled with silence and burdens. A soft knock tapped against the door, then creaked open. Jillian stepped inside quietly.

"You're awake," she said, more a statement than a question.

Derek gave a tired nod, rubbing his hands over his face. "Couldn't sleep."

She closed the door and moved toward him. "Neither could I."

For a few seconds, there was nothing but silence. Then Jillian crossed the room and sat beside him, their shoulders almost touching. "You've been holding everything in again. You don't have to. Not with me."

Derek sighed. "It's like... we're standing still, but the world keeps falling apart around us. And every time I think we've earned peace, something rips it away."

Jillian turned to him. "You're allowed to break too, you know. You don't always have to be the one fixing everything."

He didn't answer. His hands fidgeted, restless. She reached out and gently placed her hand over his. "I meant what I said before Kinross," she whispered. "I love you. I've loved you long before this world changed. And I know you love her, Derek. I'm not trying to replace that."

His eyes softened, caught between guilt and gratitude. "I don't want to hurt you."

"You're not," she said, voice firm but tender. "I'm not asking for promises. I just need you to know... I'm here. And I always will be."

There was a beat of silence, heavy with emotion. Derek finally turned to look at her fully, their faces close. The pain in his eyes was deep, but so was the comfort he found in her presence. Jillian leaned in, almost unsure, but Derek didn't pull away. Their lips met, soft, brief, more about solace than passion. A moment stolen in a world that never stopped taking.

When they pulled apart, Derek rested his forehead against hers. "I don't know what's happening to me anymore," he said quietly. "I feel like I'm splitting in half."

"You don't have to figure it all out tonight," she replied. "Just... let yourself feel something. Even if it's messy."

He nodded slowly. "Thank you, Jill." She offered a small smile.

"Get some rest. You need it." As she stood to leave, Derek caught her hand and held it for just a second longer. "I'll see you in the morning," she said.

She walked out, leaving him alone again, but this time, the weight on his shoulders didn't feel quite so heavy.

Two days later at the perimeter of Rosebank.

The trees were thick. Overgrown. Swallowing roads and buildings alike. The vehicles had been abandoned a mile back. Now it was foot travel, silent and deliberate. The team consisted of Derek, Jillian, Bellamy, Munroe, Daryl, and Maggie. The deeper they moved, the colder it became, unnaturally so.

Finally, Munroe stopped and knelt. He brushed away a pile of leaves and uncovered a slab of concrete, discolored but unmistakably man-made. A metallic symbol sat etched into its surface: the same double-helix from the notebook.

Derek's pulse quickened. "We're here."

It took them over an hour to find the entrance. Covered by debris and sealed shut with reinforced metal sheets, it was an effort to pry open. Inside, the air was stale, thick with dust and forgotten time. Flashlights illuminated a winding staircase that descended into blackness.

They entered. Inside was a lab. The walls were lined with old computer terminals, flickering monitors powered by a small backup generator still sputtering to life. Files, paper and digital, sat preserved in cases. Derek, Jillian, and Maggie split off to scan the records. Bellamy and Daryl pushed deeper. They found bodies. Skeletons dressed in white coats. But also—

"Munroe!" Bellamy called out. "Here, take a look at this." A cryogenic chamber. Sealed. Lights still active. Inside, a figure floated, suspended. A woman. Pale. Tubes running from her arms, her chest, her neck.

"Jesus," Daryl muttered. "Is she alive?"

Munroe tapped the console. "Vitals are steady. She's in stasis."

Derek arrived moments later. "Who is she?"

Bellamy stared at the nameplate. "Dr. Aria Hensley... lead scientist, Rose Bank Initiative."

They all froze.

"She was there," Maggie whispered. "From the beginning. According to the book Abby found, she was one of Ellis's top researchers."

Dr. Aria Hensley blinked against the light, breathing on her own for the first time in months.

Her voice was raspy. "You're... not Ellis," she whispered.

"No," Bellamy replied. "He's dead."

Her eyes scanned the room. "Then you don't know what's coming."

Everyone went still.

She looked directly at Derek.

"This... was only the first phase."

To be continued...

Printed in Dunstable, United Kingdom

66980092R10167